His expression was gravely enigmatic...

"You wanted six weeks for my sister-in-law to get well and make an unpressured decision," James said. "Well, I accede to your request, but there are conditions. You will take care of the children, at my farm, and you will receive a wage for your services. Do you accept?"

"I don't want money from *you*!" But Shannon's heart was lifting. The children still had a chance for the best possible life and their mother, too. Her eyes shone, then became nervous. What had changed James's mind?

"You take it or leave it, as I offered it," he persisted.

Shannon capitulated hastily. She could not jeopardize the children's chances for the sake of her own pride. "Right, I accept. But why are you doing this?"

"Not to gain *your* respect or goodwill," James answered savagely. "That's for sure!"

Run before the Wind

by

MARY MOORE

Harlequin Books

TORONTO • NEW YORK • LOS ANGELES • LONDON
AMSTERDAM • PARIS • SYDNEY • HAMBURG
STOCKHOLM • ATHENS • TOKYO • MILAN

Original hardcover edition published in 1982
by Mills & Boon Limited

ISBN 0-373-02512-2

Harlequin Romance first edition November 1982

CHAPTER ONE

SHANNON HALDANE thrust back her continental quilt and bounced out of bed. Today was her graduation day. It was Trisha's wedding day, and on Thursday, Shannon's life would be her own. For the first time in six long years she would be able to decide where she went, and what she did, and her sparkling brown eyes were alight with excitement.

She thrust the curtain aside and breathed a sigh of relief, 'Praise the Lord, a fine day! May is so unpredictable—winter just around the corner.'

The ground and lawns and flower beds were magnificent, and Trisha had been adamant that she was going to have a garden wedding. Shannon saw that the men were already erecting the huge marquee for the reception, and her eyes went soft as she saw William, her stepfather, ineffectually directing operations, and turning confusion into chaos with utmost charm.

'It must be a gift,' she smiled on her way to the shower. 'No man could be so totally impractical unless it was a gift!' Quickly she dressed, and made her bed, then flung her bridesmaid's dress and flimsy underwear on the bedspread ready for a quick change later. It was an incredibly elegant dress in crushed strawberry silk. Shannon held back the hysterical giggle that always attacked her as she imagined herself in pink, but she would happily wear sackcloth and ashes if it meant her freedom.

William had said at the rehearsal that she looked like a wild briar rose, with her small, delicate-boned face and olive skin. Of course, Marsha and Cushla, with beautiful blonde hair and peaches and cream complexions identical to Trisha's, looked fantastic. They were tall, they had naturally curly hair, they were adorable, her three young stepsisters, and each one had insisted on having her for a bridesmaid when they married. It was their way of showing love, even though she looked such an oddity with her short dark straight hair and definite lack of inches.

'Three times a bridesmaid, never a bride,' she sang happily as she raced down the stairs and out to join her stepfather.

'Am I glad to see you! These fellows have no idea where to place the main table. In fact, I would say they're totally incompetent.'

'Good morning!' smiled Shannon. 'Isn't it fantastic, having a fine day? Come along inside and I'll make you a nice breakfast, then I'll take some up to Trisha.'

'But what about the arrangements here, Shannon?' he protested halfheartedly. 'I should keep an eye on things.'

'No, that's exactly what you should not do. It will only upset you. You trusted me with all the organisation, and I have everything at my fingertips. Now relax!'

He pushed his glasses back on his nose, then looked over the top of them a little anxiously. 'You're sure?'

'Positive,' said Shannon with a smile.

'How do you cope, Shannon? You're such a little thing. And how am I going to manage without you?'

'Wonderfully well,' Shannon assured him, although her heart smote her at his forlorn look. Then she hardened herself. If she stayed on she was going to spoil William's only chance of a happy marriage. He had had two most unfortunate experiences, and Catherine would be a wonderful wife for him.

As she turned the sizzling bacon and slipped the

eggs into the frying pan, her mind kept turning to the phrase, graduation day. Sure, the others had graduated from nursing school, teachers' college, and university, and her graduation carried no diploma. Five years ago, at seventeen, she had promised her mother that she would take care of the three girls, until they married or left home to live their own lives.

Well, she had kept her promise, and it had not been easy. For five years she had devoted herself to her stepfather and the girls, and had never spared a thought for her own plans, but now she was free, and she intended to stay that way. No man would ever trap her into marriage. No matter how interesting he was, no matter how attractive he was, he would have nothing to offer to compare with letting her be captain of her own life, and that included Simon.

'What's going to happen to me?' her stepfather asked a little pettishly as she slid his breakfast in front of him. 'You've done everything for me since your mother died. I've often felt it was unfair to let you, but there seemed to be no alternative.'

'There wasn't.' Shannon's slightly crooked grin gave her face an impish appeal. 'But there is now. A fine scholarly gentleman such as yourself, with a magnificent residence to offer, should have no trouble choosing himself a loving wife to cheer his declining years.'

William peered over his glasses and frowned. 'You know my opinion of marriage. It coincides with your own. How dare you suggest I stick my neck back in the noose?'

Shannon giggled. 'You're a wicked old man! There you are, planning quite enthusiastically to hand your darling youngest daughter over to the bliss of matrimony in a couple of hours, and at the same time avoiding the fate yourself. Shocking! No, you're just a bad picker. This time I'll choose your wife, and she'll look after you much better than I could.'

'That's not possible. Can't we go on just the same as we always have? Or is that selfish of me to suggest?'

'It is,' Shannon replied as she set Trisha's tray neatly and started for the stairs. 'Aren't you interested to know who I've chosen?'

'No. It's ridiculous,' he harrumphed. 'Who did you have in mind?'

She chuckled and yelled from the top of the stairs, 'Frances, of course!'

The next few hours kaleidoscoped into beautiful and varied patterns of guests arriving, presents being opened and displayed, the girls getting dressed, and the bride, Trisha, arrayed in all her glory, coming down the stairs on her father's arm. What a picture she made!

The wedding service was simple, yet keeping the age old promises, 'to have and to hold, from this day forward' . . . Shannon brushed away an unexpected tear, and was annoyed to see that Simon was watching. He could put whatever interpretation he liked on her unusual surrender to sentimentality, but the fact was that she had stood in a mother's place to the girls even though they were only a couple of years younger than herself, and Trisha was the youngest, the baby . . . so she was *entitled* to her tears.

At last the reception and the toasts were over and she helped Trisha dress in her going-away outfit.

'I hope you'll always be as happy as you are today, Trish, love.'

'I will be. Barney and I are made for each other. Give me my bouquet, Shannon—there's someone very special I want to catch it.' She flung her arms around Shannon's neck. 'I love you. I don't know how to thank you for all you've done today to make this wedding day absolutely perfect, and for all the other days you've looked after Cushla and Marsha and me. Now we're all married, and within a year. It seems incredible! I feel such a beast, going off to live an exciting life with Barney and leaving you travelling along, and Dad here, stuck in the same old routine. It doesn't seem fair. But you will marry Simon?'

Shannon neatly evaded the question.

'Now, no tears. I'm delighted to see you all married off. I thought I'd have you on my hands for years.'

She kissed Trisha's lovely flushed face and pushed her out of the door into Barney's impatient arms.

'You're coming down to wave us off?' Trisha called anxiously.

'Sure am.' Shannon cast an eye over the mess in the room and firmly closed the door on it. She would tidy it up later. She followed the laughing couple down the stairs, thankful that it was a morning wedding and hoping the guests would soon drift away. That would leave her the afternoon to put everything straight for the last time, and then she would leave on the ferry tonight for the South Island.

At the car, she found Simon beside her, while Trisha and her husband were being showered with confetti.

'Okay, Trish—now!' Simon called, and Shannon felt his arms go round her and her hands imprisoned in his as the bride's bouquet flew through the air towards them, and found herself unwillingly clutching it.

'You beast! You planned that with Trish!' Shannon spluttered.

'Never. It was a purely spontaneous action. I saw you were yearning to have it, so I just helped you. Remember what it means ... you'll be the next bride.' He kissed her enthusiastically.

'Not yours, anyway,' Shannon snapped furiously. 'That was a despicable trick!'

Simon grinned down at her, completely unrepentant. 'Wave, they're leaving.'

Shannon turned to speed them on their way, then returned to argue with Simon. 'Ha! The bouquet means nothing, but it's a proven fact that three times a bridesmaid, never a bride, so I'm quite safe.'

'With your face and figure, you'll never be safe. Men will always be pestering you to marry them. So why not accept me, and save yourself a lot of trouble?'

'Marriage, death and taxes, and the worst of these is marriage.' Shannon was laughing again. 'My sentiments exactly.'

'You can't mean that, Shannon. You've just engineered the third wedding from this house this year, and William tells me you're already planning his doom. I thought you loved him. Frances will eat him alive and you know it.' His handsome face creased into an attractive smile. 'Marry me and I'll even consider moving in here so you can still wet-nurse the old duck.'

'No. You're both on your own. I tried to get William to accept a housekeeper, and he wouldn't, so Frances it is.' Her grin widened. 'I'm off south tonight. You'll soon find someone else to console you. I've told you all along, I'm not ever going to get married. . . .'

'That's just a phase you're going through. Take a month off on your holiday, and I'll guarantee you won't find anyone who'll suit you better than I will.

We get along fine. Go on, admit it.'

'Sure. I have no trouble admitting that if I had any intention of getting married, you'd be my choice. You're quite gorgeous to look at, you've got a fantastic sense of humour, you're hardworking, intelligent, and compared to me, filthy rich, but marriage means sharing, and I'm not prepared to share. It's that simple. I want to belong to me, make my own decisions, be free.'

'Yet you're quite pleased that the girls have married?'

Shannon shrugged her slim shoulders in a more than eloquent manner. 'They're suited to marriage . . . I'm not. You know that old saying about greatness: some are born great, some achieve greatness and some have it thrust upon them. Well, marriage is like that. I was not born to it, I don't want to achieve it, and I've no intention of having it thrust upon me.'

'You'll change your mind,' Simon said confidently. 'I'll wait.'

'It'll be a long wait.'

'Not as long as you think. Remember, it's better to marry than burn.'

'I'll call the Fire Brigade,' she assured him with a chuckle. 'Now I'm off to find William.'

'You're a hardhearted wench. Will you have dinner with me before leaving on the ferry?'

'Love to, provided you promise not to propose again.'

'Can't promise—it's become a habit. I see you're still clutching the bouquet, which probably shows an unconscious desire to become a bride.'

She flung it at him and when he fielded it skilfully, she tried to avoid having it thrust back in her hands.

'You shouldn't wear pink, Shannon,' he told her.

'Let me go! Why?'

'Pink is for sweet, loving, feminine little girls, the sort a man can tuck under his arm.'

'You mean keep under his thumb,' she replied mischievously, and disappeared through the crowd of departing guests.

She found her stepfather hiding in his study enjoying a quiet pipe. 'Have they all gone?' he asked.

'Almost. Would you like a cup of tea?'

'Yes.' He peered over his spectacles. 'And don't tell that awful female where I am! She's hounded me all afternoon, like a vulture moving in on a dying animal.'

'You mean Frances. She'd make you an excellent wife.' Shannon stopped at the door. 'You absolutely refused to have a housekeeper. You're incapable of looking after yourself, you admit that, and I'm not staying, so there's only Frances.'

'She would make me give up smoking, and said as much this afternoon. Said I'd live longer. Married to her, why would I want to live longer?'

Shannon chuckled. 'Oh, it doesn't have to be her, but she is available, and although it's not delicate to mention it, more than willing—you sexy old thing, you! You're incredibly attractive, William, and there's probably dozens of nurses at the hospital just longing to get off with darling Doc Travers, but you don't even see them, do you? You're an orthopaedic specialist, a real bone man, and all you know or are interested in is bones, and chess. Nurses are a bit like players who hand you things, point you in the right direction and give you your patients' names. Go on, you couldn't even name one of the women you work with. See, it's got to be Frances. She's been your secretary for ages and has been. . . .'

'*I will not marry Frances.*' William pushed his glasses back and glared at Shannon. 'And I can remember the nurses!'

'Name one,' Shannon taunted.

'Catherine,' William announced triumphantly.

'You mean your Theatre Sister, the redheaded one?'

'No, she's not redheaded,' William pushed his glasses back again impatiently. 'She's small, about your height, dark hair, kind eyes, so kind. I think they're blue . . . and good legs, essential that, good legs.'

'Essential,' Shannon concurred, straight-faced, but her brown eyes were dancing with delight. She had been right, William had more than noticed his beautiful Theatre Sister. 'She wouldn't be any good as your wife, she'd spoil you horribly, let you have all your own way, never burn your revolting old gardening pants and cardigans and slippers.'

William's smile was pure delight, 'You're absolutely correct, she would be easy on the mind. I bet she wouldn't even nag me about smoking. We've got a lot in common, Catherine and I . . . why, I'm always surprised how swiftly time passes when I share a coffee with her . . . she has a fine mind and a dry sense of humour.'

'Sorry, William, it's got to be Frances,' Shannon said decisively.

'What's wrong with Catherine? She can play chess.'

'Not a thing. It's just that I know you. Frances already scents victory . . . and she'll have you at the altar before you know it. You let women bully you, William. Your first wife caught you while you were still at medical college, and not really ready for the responsibility of marriage. You told me so yourself. She gave you three daughters, and one hell of a life, then cleared off and left you. Then you let your family talk you into writing to my mother and offering her a home with you when her marriage broke up. She married you, and dominated you until she died, the same way she treated my dad until he up and left.'

'Your mother was good to me, and great with the girls,' William protested.

'Because it suited her,' Shannon said grimly. 'Did you fall in love with her, William? Did you ask her to marry you, William? Or did it just happen, because she thought it a sensible arrangement?'

William shrugged his shoulders a little hopelessly, and puffed on his pipe. 'You know me too well, Shannon . . . and you're bullying me.'

'Well, it's in a good cause. You've been master of your own home for the first time in your life, these last five years. I'm disgusted to think you'll allow Frances to drag you unprotestingly into marriage, and then proceed to shape you up her way, when with a little effort you could have Catherine as a tender loving companion beside you.'

'What sort of effort?' William demanded cautiously.

'More than you're capable of!' Shannon shouted fiercely. 'It would mean courting her, ringing her up and asking her out to dinner, sending her flowers, taking her to the ballet, or the theatre, a sustained effort . . . too much for you, William. Frances will gobble you up, like a sitting duck, or worm.'

She was surprised to find she had to brush away her tears as she waited for the kettle to boil. Tears twice in one day . . . she must be getting soft! She resented the pain she was feeling at leaving home. Her stepfather knew that she planned to leave immediately after the wedding . . . she couldn't give up her plans for freedom . . . yet she hated to abandon him to Frances. She could shake him, he was a procrastinator. Yet he had given her a home from the age of eleven . . . more than a home, he had given love. She had been a thin dark child, angry and still grieving for her father, and William, who had never been able to understand or communicate with his own girls, had suddenly been completely and entirely captivated by her. He had described her as 'all mouth and eyes' like a small wild thing trapped in an alien environment. It had been a strange friendship, and almost from the beginning she had become his fierce protector against her mother's domineering nature. And now she was leaving him to fend for himself.

She prepared the tray and marched back into the study. He was putting her in an absolutely untenable position. He knew that she was close to being fanatical about people running their own lives. If it was a backlash against the way her mother swallowed people whole, feeling herself perfectly capable of running her own life and everyone else's, did it matter?

She poured the tea and sat down opposite him. 'I'm leaving tonight,' she announced.

'What about Simon?'

'Look, you run your life, I'll run mine.' She sipped her tea. 'I'm sorry if I seemed to be bullying you before—about Frances, I mean. It's just that I hate to see you so *weak*. You're a first-class surgeon, an eminent lecturer at the medical school, with your own list of private patients, and you're clear, decisive and intelligent regarding every aspect of your profession, yet you're such a gorgeous duffer about your personal life. You just let things happen. I love you . . . but you're making me feel such a beast for leaving you.'

An amused smile lit his face. 'Okay, I'll admit I've been trying to make you feel that way, because quite frankly I abhor change. You've made me too comfortable. But it's time to admit to a little deception. I always knew deep down you'd fly away, and the thought of Frances has driven me to think of the awful consequences of playing target. While you were out I rang Catherine, and I'm taking her out to dinner. Does that ease your mind?'

Shannon flew out of her chair to hug him. 'Oh, you just don't know how happy it's made me!'

'Right, I'll add a little more. I've been incredibly devious over the past few months while you've been in a turmoil over the wedding. I've been seeing quite a lot of Catherine, and we're going to be married. I've kept it secret for several reasons. I thought that maybe you would be hurried from your nest if I told you, and I wouldn't have that, this is your home. Again, I thought Simon might win if I gave you a little more time, so I played poor defenceless man to keep you pinned down. I like that young man, but you're not going to marry him, are you?'

'No, I'm not, and he's always known it. You are sneaky! I can't believe you managed all this on your own. Oh, William, you *are* doing it because you want to, not because you . . .?'

'Are choosing the softest option?' he chuckled. 'You really do know me well! For a start, maybe, that was in my mind, but I think for the first time in my life I've fallen in love, and I can't wait for you all to clear out so that I can bring her home.'

Shannon felt the last silken bonds of responsibility slip from her. She had loved this family and William most of all, and had been so worried for him.

The rest of the afternoon rushed by and at dinner she tried to match Simon's mood of sad farewell, but failed utterly. She was free, she was free, she was free! Her own person.

Restlessly she wandered the deck of the ferry as it moved down the Wellington Harbour, loving the lights on the water, enjoying the fresh warm breeze against her cheeks, not trying to quieten the new song of freedom that was singing in her heart. She didn't want to sit in the lounge, or talk to anyone, or even plan ahead, but to enjoy this moment to the full.

Perhaps she should have made plans for her life, but she never had. She had never looked beyond this moment when, free from entanglements, she would roam where she pleased. 'Run before the wind,' her father had told her when he left home. 'Let it blow you where it will, and enjoy every part of it.'

How she had loved him! He had been her whole world. Others had called him careless, selfish, irresponsible, but to her he had been a king. She had only been nine when he left. She would never forget the night he had come to her room, and said goodbye. He had taken her in his arms and told her she was the only thing worthwhile in his life, the only part that had made life bearable, but as much as he loved her, he could not endure another day of suburbia, and a nine-to-five existence. He had promised to write to her wherever he travelled, and when she was old enough he would send for her and they would roam the world together.

Shannon sighed. He had kept his promise, and then when she was eleven her mother had received word he had been killed in a glider accident in Canada, and her whole world seemed to come apart. That was when they moved to Wellington and lived with William and the girls. But always she had been waiting for this moment, and now it had arrived. She had a good bank account—William had always been generous. She had her little car. She would have a good look around the South Island, then head overseas. And then she'd keep travelling, working a little when the opportunity occurred, moving on when the mood took her, just the way it would have been if her father had lived.

Yet she was a little different from him, because she liked people.

His favourite saying had been that the world was a beautiful place, except for the people who lived in it. He had warned her to keep her life uncluttered, not to get involved. It would only slow her down. Well, she would be careful in future.

She had a cup of coffee, then went to the observation lounge, and found a vacant seat. There were not many people travelling on the late ferry. It wouldn't arrive in Picton until midnight, so most people went on the daylight trips. She would also have loved to see the Sounds in daylight, but it would have been a bit callous to refuse Simon's invitation. Her lips curved into an unconscious smile as she remembered his cunning lawyer-like arguments to get her tied down to some commitment before she left. He had been fun to get round with, but he was only a good friend. She had promised to think about him while she was away, but that was all.

Her attention was drawn to the slight figure of a girl about her own age sitting not far from her. The girl was so frail, with a pallor that denoted recent illness, her fair hair framing a face of incredible beauty, and she had a small lively girl of three or four with her to control. There was a tiredness and apathy in her whole demeanour that spoke of total exhaustion, yet now and again she would turn restlessly towards the sea, searching almost as if she was looking for a landmark, a look of desperation on her face.

Shannon had twice already carefully refrained from offering her help, and it was silly to feel guilty about it. After all, there were stewards about, if the girl needed help. She knew what was holding her back, and that rankled. It was that silly observation Simon had made at dinner, that she did not know herself at all. In spite of seeing herself as a free roving spirit, at heart she was someone who needed roots.

He had said, 'You're so busy proving that you're not like your mother that you haven't realised that you have very little of your father in you either. You have an open heart for every lame dog that ever crossed your path. You're a loving, caring, totally involved person, involved with anyone and everyone who has some misfortune. Far from moving high, wide and handsome through life, selfishly living your own way, you'll be hooked into someone else's problem before the week is out. If you were like your father you wouldn't have stayed five years with William and the girls. You would have callously abandoned them, just as your father opted out of his responsibilities. You need someone to protect you from yourself . . . and that someone is me.'

She had grinned back at him, pretending that his remarks about her father had not hurt, and knowing he had only been trying to sway her to his point of view. Still, it had shaken her, because she knew that he was a very clever and astute lawyer, and she had always respected his judgment of people. Of course she knew he was wrong about *her*, but his remarks had penetrated deeply enough to make her hesitant about going to speak to the girl.

The girl turned, as if knowing she was being observed, and stared directly at Shannon, despair and indecision written openly on her features. Then, suddenly coming to a decision, she got up from her seat, holding the heavy baby sleeping in her arms. She called the little girl and walked towards Shannon.

'I have to go to the restrooms. Would you mind keeping Marigold? I can't manage both of them.' Her voice was soft and pleading.

'Certainly.' Shannon gave her a reassuring smile. 'Come on, Marigold, hop up beside me.' She lifted the unsmiling child into the vacant seat beside her.

The mother stood staring at them as if she had drifted off into some dream world of her own, and had forgotten that she was going anywhere.

Shannon leaned forward and touched her arm. 'I'll keep the baby as well, if you like.'

'No, you're not having Joshua. Nobody's having Joshua. I'm taking him with me.' And she rushed away.

Her manner and aggressive response had startled Shannon, who stared after her in surprise before turning to the little girl. 'Your name is Marigold, isn't it? My, that's a pretty name. I've never met any one called Marigold before.'

Marigold stared back suspiciously.

Shannon hastily searched her bag and found a large packet of jellybeans which Simon had given her, knowing her great weakness for them. She handed the packet to Marigold.

The little girl handled them carefully, then looked up at Shannon uncertainly. 'Are they all for me?'

'Yes, love, they're all yours. Do you want me to help you open them?'

'No, I can do it.' She worked diligently on the tough package until she got one corner open, then thoughtfully extracted two, neatly folded over the corner, and chewed her sweets silently.

Shannon kept quiet, thinking it was better not to talk in case Marigold was shy.

After a few minutes Marigold turned to her with a grin, as if she had decided anyone who handed out large packets of jellybeans couldn't be all bad. 'My daddy called me Marigold. He's in heaven now.'

A little taken aback, Shannon said, 'I'm sorry to hear that.'

Marigold shook her head impatiently. 'It's not *bad*. Mummy says he gets to sing with Jesus every day.'

'And that's good?' Shannon asked.

'Yes. But just sometimes I wish he wasn't so happy, and would come back and play with us.' She turned her attention back to her sweets, not seeing the quick compassion on Shannon's face.

Again she took two sweets, and meticulously rolled up the corner of the package. Shannon watched, intrigued. There was something heartcatching about the quaint little girl.

Marigold stood up on the seat and looked towards the sea. 'That water out there is very deep. Do you think it's very, very deep?'

Shannon looked out to the dark heaving sea, and agreed. 'Very, very deep indeed.'

Marigold gave her a mischievous smile. 'Bet Jesus couldn't walk on that water.'

'Oh, I think he could,' Shannon said firmly. 'He can do anything.'

Marigold was silent for quite a long time. 'Then I'm going to keep looking, because I might see him.' She turned her head on one side in a birdlike movement. 'You see, Mummy's going to go to Heaven too.'

'I'm sure she is,' Shannon agreed again, wondering a little at the strange conversation. 'But not for a long time. She's got to look after you and Joshua.'

'She's taking Joshua with her.' Marigold gave her a disapproving look. 'That's why she wouldn't let you nurse him.'

Shannon gasped as she realised the implication. 'You mean now!'

'Yes. I'm big, but he's too little. . . .'

Shannon was on her feet in an instant, completely alert now to the sick girl's strange behaviour. As a steward went by she caught his arm. 'Stay with this child till I get back.'

She gave him no chance to argue, but headed for the door through which the mother and baby had disappeared. Perhaps she should have raised the alarm, but she *could* be wrong. Something deep inside told her she wasn't wrong, and she ran the length of the gangway to the darkened end of the ship.

There was no one about at the bow of the ship, and she stood there searching the water sliding past and seeing the islands dark and shadowy around her.

A movement along the deck made her turn, sharply aware, and she saw the shape of the young slender girl outlined by the light. She saw the girl bend down and pick up the child where it must have been placed asleep at her feet, and in that instant Shannon knew.

She stood frozen, watching the girl, throwing a glance back, climb on the rail and balance herself, then swing the baby over her shoulder, before the leap. Shannon rushed forward and jerked the two of them backwards on to the deck, shouting rather foolishly, 'What the hell are you trying to do?'

The girl huddled crying on the deck and Shannon picked up the heavy child and comforted it. In mid-yell it stopped, and beamed at her. It was a gorgeous-looking child of about one year old.

Shannon's heart was still thudding with the fright she had received, and she looked around a bit wildly to see if there was anyone who could help her, but the deck was empty. She was scared to go for help in case the girl got up and hurled herself over the rail while she was away, and she was appalled to find she did not want to get involved in whatever was going on.

'Here, sit up—come on, I'll help you. Look, I'm sorry if I hurt you.' Shannon thought that was about the most idiotic thing she could have said. What were a few bruises? The stranger could have been drowned by now if she had not grabbed her. Oh, damn, what a mess! 'What's the baby's name? He's a cute kid.

How could you do such a thing? You nearly scared me to death!' Again the unfortunate choice of words struck and made her even angrier. 'Look, get up and stop crying. I'll get some help. Things can't be as bad as you think.'

At those words the girl got up shakily, 'Please, please, don't tell anyone. Please just give me Joshua, and leave me alone. I'm sorry I frightened you, but it was the only answer. Please don't tell anyone!'

Shannon stared at her, feeling all her anger drain away. The girl was hardly more than a child herself, with tear-filled blue eyes and fair hair, and pale beyond description. 'Okay, it's all right, I won't call anyone. You look ill and cold. Come along to the lounge and I'll get you a hot cup of coffee, and you can tell me all about it. I'll try and understand, really I will.'

'No, I'm not going anywhere. Just give me Joshua, and leave us alone.'

Shannon's grip on the baby tightened as she asked grimly, 'If I do are you going to jump overboard again?'

'Yes.'

'Don't be so crazy,' Shannon said impatiently. 'What's your name? Tell me your name.'

'Michelle McCabe.' Her tone was desperate but still determined.

'Well, Michelle, I'll give you two choices. Either you come along for that coffee, or I'll hang on to you and yell my hezd off till someone comes to help me. Take your pick.'

'What right have you to interfere in my life?' Michaelle knuckled her tears away.

'None. And I wish you'd timed your exit more carefully. But you didn't, and we're stuck with each other,' Shannon answered crisply. 'Are you coming?'

'Have your own way, then, but I've got no money.

My purse fell into the sea, but there wasn't anything in it anyway. Where's Marigold?'

'With a steward—don't worry about her, or money. I'll pay.' Shannon shifted Joshua on to her other hip and shepherded Michelle ahead of her, breathing a sigh of relief as she got her into the lighted room and sat her down at the table. She went over and got a cup of hot soup and also some coffee. There seemed nothing she could get the baby as the service hatch was closed and only the vending machine open.

She watched Michelle shaking uncontrollably as she tried to drink the soup, and wondered what on earth she was going to do next.

As if reading her mind the girl stared at her apprehensively. 'You promised you wouldn't tell anyone.'

Shannon couldn't remember whether she had promised or not, but if she had Michelle wasn't the only one out of her mind. She had to have help. She had to hand these three over to some authority who knew how to deal with the problem.

'Where are you heading?' she asked. 'Where were you going when you got to Picton? You must have planned on staying somewhere.'

'I wasn't going to reach Picton. If you hadn't interfered. . . .'

'Oh, do shut up!' Shannon snapped impatiently. 'Will you let me take you to a doctor there? Look, Michelle, you've got to have help.'

'No, I won't go to a doctor. I won't go to the police. I won't go to Welfare—I've been there, and they can't help. Nobody can help.'

Shannon panicked as she heard the rising hysteria in Michelle's voice. 'It's all right. It's all right, Michelle. I've booked a motel, so there'll be room for us all. Will you stay with me? If you promise me you'll behave yourself, and spend the night with me, I won't tell anyone what's happened, but if you're going to do something stupid again, then I'll ask to speak to the captain.'

Instantly the fight went out of Michelle. 'Okay, but I told you I've got no money.'

Relieved, Shannon drew a deep breath. 'That's good. I promise you that after a good sleep things won't look so bad. I'll help you sort out whatever's troubling you, Trust me.'

Michelle looked at her sadly. 'I know you mean well, but no one can sort this out. You've just ruined the perfect answer.'

An aggrieved-looking steward appeared at the table, holding a bag in one hand and Marigold in the other. 'That's a bit much, pushing your kid on to me while you sit here calmly drinking tea!' He dropped the bag on the floor. 'She wouldn't come unless I brought the bag. I hope it belongs to you.'

'Thank you,' Shannon said sweetly, making no attempt to defend her action. 'You've been very kind. Sit here by me, Marigold. Have you still got your jellybeans? Good, perhaps you'll give Joshua one.'

'I'll give him two,' Marigold said seriously.

Shannon hid a grin and said to Michelle, 'She's a darling kid. She isn't afraid of strangers . . . well, not if they have sweets.'

Michaelle said bitterly, 'How could she be afraid? Strangers have had the care of her more than I have since Joshua was born. I've been ill, and she was taken into care. She's come through it all marvellously, that's why I knew she was a survivor. But when they said they were taking Joshua—well, I knew I couldn't give him up. . . .'

The tears flowed down her pale cheeks and she made no attempt to wipe them away.

'Why would they take him?' Shannon asked.

'Because I'm incompetent. Because I'm an inadequate mother. Oh, I know what they say is true.

Mark's brother would give them a wonderful life, but I want my own children.'

'I'm sure you do, and you seem to be managing all right to me.' It wasn't true but Shannon wanted to get them all safely off the ferry. After a good night's sleep she would try and help Michelle sort things out. She was sure things weren't as bad as the girl imagined. It was ridiculous to think her children would be taken away just because she was ill.

By the time she had them all bedded down at the motel she was very tired. Fortunately the proprietors were still up, and changed her accommodation to fit the size of the party, and included a cot for Joshua. Shannon thought she'd fall into bed and asleep in the same breath, but her mind kept churning over and over the few things Michelle had volunteered before she fell asleep. And what if she woke up during the night and decided to carry out her intention?

Shannon lay wide awake, glad that Simon had no knowledge of her present predicament. And she'd see he never knew. The whole thing had to be settled tomorrow. Michelle had said so. She had said her husband's brother had offered to take the children, but she was never to have any contact with them for the rest of their lives. It was monstrous. And he'd given her three months to decide, and tomorrow was the last day. What a brute he must be! No wonder Michelle had been almost driven out of her mind. Well, he now had two to reckon with, and Shannon felt she was more than a match for such a despicable creature. She tried to recall his name. James, that was it—James McCabe.

Well, James McCabe, she thought, I may forget your name, but when I meet you tomorrow you'll have good cause to remember mine. Ruining my first day of freedom!

CHAPTER TWO

SEVERAL times during the night Shannon went to check on Michelle and found her sleeping deeply. It was such a relief. Then the children had woken crying, and she had gone in and covered them and comforted them and they had slept again. Towards morning she fell into an exhausted sleep and the morning sun streaming in the window wakened her.

She glanced at her watch—'Whoops, nine o'clock!' It was only then she became aware of Marigold standing by her bed, watching her intently, her slight frame clad in knickers and singlet.

'Good morning, Marigold. Have you been waiting for me to wake up?'

Marigold nodded.

Shannon pushed back the bedclothes and sat on the edge of the bed. Something about the child's forlorn expression caught at her heart, and she was surprised to hear herself say, 'Are you too big to have a cuddle?'

Marigold shrugged her thin shoulders. 'I don't think so.'

Shannon reached out and scooped her on to her knee. 'Goodness me, you're as light as a feather! I think Joshua is heavier than you.'

For a few moments Marigold sat stiffly resisting her arms, then suddenly relaxed almost bonelessly against her, and again Shannon was surprised at the warmth of her love for the small pixie-faced girl, with her wide, blue, slightly almond-shaped eyes. She stroked the fine soft brown hair and tried to steel herself against the surge of protective feeling that swept her. She was not going to get involved with this family. Just today she would give to help them along, then they'd be on their own. She had her life to live and no matter how shocked she felt about their circumstances, she had to remember there were agencies and people geared to help. It was stupid to feel responsible for them.

Marigold nestled closer. 'Do you know any stories?'

'Not many,' Shannon admitted. 'I don't know any children much at all. What sort of stories?'

'Mark used to tell me stories. Mummy doesn't have time.' There was no condemnation in the tone, just a statement.

'Who's Mark?'

'My daddy—you know, I told you. He's up in Heaven.' She twisted round so that she could watch Shannon's eyes. 'Are you going to Heaven?'

There was an unconscious appeal for reassurance, a fear barely hidden, yet a resignation and loneliness that was far beyond her years, and Shannon reacted with a fierce hug. 'Some day, but not for years and years and years.'

She was rewarded with an enchanting, sparkling-eyed grin. 'Ooooh, I'm glad! I like the stories of the Three Little Pigs,' she added. 'Will you tell me one?'

Shannon stretched backwards into her memory bank and started off hesitantly, 'Once upon a time, there were three little pigs. . . .'

Marigold snuggled down with a contented sigh. 'That's the one.'

Somehow she pieced the whole story together with considerable help from Marigold, and ended on a triumphant note, 'And that was the end of the Big Bad Wolf, and the three little pigs lived happily ever after. Was that good?'

'Not as good as Mark,' Marigold said carefully.

'Huh! I get better with practice,' Shannon laughed, then stood up and dropped Marigold on the bed. 'You're a tough boss.' She rolled the little girl in the bedclothes and tickled her. Above the laughter came a determined yell from the other bedroom.

'That's Joshua!' announced Marigold.

'It is indeed. What happens now?'

'He has a bottle.' Marigold rushed through to the room and came back with an empty bottle, which she handed up to Shannon.

'I don't know anything about babies,' Shannon said a little grimly. 'Still, there's milk in the fridge. I suppose I have to heat it. Isn't your mummy awake?'

'No.' Marigold had hurried to the fridge and was holding out the milk to her. 'He doesn't have it hot.'

Shannon ran her hand through her hair. 'Well, I guess I'm lucky to have you to help.' She rinsed the bottle and filled it, then went into the room. Joshua stopped crying and met her with a beaming smile. 'You're a handsome boy, aren't you, Joshua?' She lifted him out and, after a glance at Michelle who was still asleep, took him through to her own bed and put him down with the bottle.

'You'll have to change him,' Marigold informed her. 'His nappies are in our bag.'

'You learn something new every day,' Shannon muttered, and fetched the bag, relieved to find the nappies already folded. At least she could see how the wet ones were attached, and felt quite a sense of achievement as she neatly pinned on the new one and pulled on the plastic pants. 'What next?'

Marigold burrowed in the bag. 'A clean top.' She

handed it to Shannon. 'And these pants. If you're quick, you dress him before he finishes his bottle or he'll yell.'

'Heaven forbid!' Shannon felt so clumsy, but finally had him dressed, even with socks and wee sandals. 'There you go, now what about you?'

Marigold scrunched up her face. 'My top is dirty.'

'Haven't you got another one?'

Again the so expressive shrug of the shoulders. 'No, Mummy just took me from the house with no clothes. She said the lady might not let me go.'

Shannon wondered how many years you got for kidnapping. Could you kidnap your own child? 'Show me your top,' she said.

Marigold brought it with such a look of disdain. 'It's dirty.'

'It sure is,' Shannon agreed. 'Tell you what, we'll nip across to the shops and buy a clean one. Would you like that? Or a dress, perhaps?'

'A whole dress?' Marigold was amazed.

'No, stupid, half a dress.' Shannon chuckled. 'Which half will you have? Top half, or bottom half?'

Marigold giggled helplessly, and it was a beautiful sound.

'Is Joshua all right while I have a shower? I'll be quick. We'll have to buy something for breakfast too. What do you eat?' Shannon gathered up her clothes and headed for the bathroom. Joshua seemed happy lifting the pedal bin lid and dropping it with a satisfying bang. He could hardly hurt himself there.

The shower refreshed her wonderfully and she dressed in jeans and a silky skivvy. It looked like being a hot day. 'Look, you'll have to wear that top. . . .'

'No, I won't,' Marigold looked mutinous. 'It's dirty!'

'Well, come as you are. You're a bit young to be run in for indecent exposure.'

'I'll put my shorts on,' Marigold offered generously, having won her point.

'Great! I'll check on your mother.' Shannon stood by the bed, and for a moment was scared that the still, pale figure was not breathing. It shook her badly, and she hesitated about going to the shops. What if Michelle woke up and found the children gone? What if she woke up still determined to kill herself? Well, she would just have to chance it. The children needed food. Come to think of it, she was starving herself.

Briskly she left the room and hefting Joshua on her hip, picked up her purse. In answer to Marigold's questioning glance she said, 'Your mother is still asleep. I'm a bit worried about leaving her. . . .'

Marigold led the way to the door. 'Jesus will look after her. Let's go and buy the dress.'

'I wish I had half your faith, chicken,' Shannon sighed as she followed the little girl out to the car. Obviously buying a dress was a tremendous event in her life. Shannon drove the short distance to the shops, and ignoring Marigold's pleas first purchased groceries. 'Bread, butter, honey, milk, eggs—what else do we need?'

'Me and Joshua always eat weetbix, and we have Marmite on toast.' Marigold picked them off the shelf and dropped them into the cart, where Joshua happily started to demolish them. 'And sometimes Mummy gives us chocolate and fizzy drink.'

'Good try,' Shannon chuckled. 'But not for breakfast.' She paid for the items and managed to get them and Joshua back to the car. 'You weigh a ton,

Joshua McCabe! Would he be all right if we left him to buy the dress? It's just next door.'

Marigold shook her head emphatically. 'He'll yell.'

Shannon sighed and lowered him to the sidewalk, then pushed the bag into the car, turning to find Joshua with a cigarette stub just disappearing into his baby mouth. With difficulty she extracted it, observing nervously, 'He's got sharp teeth.' She gave him a quick kiss as a reward for giving up his treasure without amputating her fingers, and he grinned amiably at her. He really was a darling.

Marigold was well ahead of her going into the shop and headed straight for a rack of children's frocks, a blissful look on her face.

When the attendant came along Shannon explained their predicament and the girl cheerfully lifted down several attractive dresses. Marigold eyed each offering intently, then slowly shook her head.

'Oh, here's one you'll love,' said the girl, choosing a pretty lacy model with pink ribbons. 'Just the right size, too.'

'No,' Marigold said firmly. 'Not that one.'

'Come on, Marigold,' Shannon said impatiently, 'we haven't got all day.' She was surprised at the little girl's careful scrutiny and rather intrigued at her decisive manner, but Joshua was squirming vigorously and she was anxious to get back to Michelle. She put him down for a moment. 'Look, love, you'll have to pick one of these, they're the only ones in your size.'

Marigold fingered each frock again, and shook her head doubtfully.

The attendant laughed, 'My word, she has definite tastes! Oh, we do have two more out the back, maybe they'll please her.' She hurried away.

'Look, choose a new top, at least. You can't continue to run round in your singlet.' Shannon moved to another counter and rescued Joshua from another rubbish container. 'You're going to be a garbage collector when you grow up—I can tell.'

A man passing by laughed at her. 'He's got the makings of an All-Black, that one!'

Shannon grinned, 'He's big enough now. He takes a lot of stopping.' She turned back to Marigold who had a pretty yellow top in her hand.

'This one, please.'

'Thank goodness!' Shannon removed the ticket and pulled it over Marigold's head, just as the assistant came back with three dresses.

'Ah!' Marigold's eyes filled with genuine delight. 'This one,' she said softly, touching a plain little blue dress with white piping. 'It's lovely.'

She stood quietly while it was measured against her, and Shannon had to admit the simple frock suited her far better than any of the frilled and be-ribboned ones that she had passed over.

'We'll take it, and this top, and singlet and two pair of knickers—anything will do.'

As the assistant went to wrap up the purchase, Marigold tugged Shannon's hand anxiously and whispered, 'Have you got enough money?'

'Yes, dear, I've got plenty.'

Marigold's face lit with joy. 'Mummy never has. She gives all hers to the milkman.' She insisted on carrying the parcel and danced ahead of Shannon out to the car.

Shannon followed more slowly, comparing the swirling little body and excited flushed face with the forlorn wee girl who had stood by her bed earlier. What a small price to pay for such happiness! Poor Michelle, how hard it must be not to have any money to indulge even occasionally in buying a new dress for her daughter. Then again that inner voice warned her, 'Don't get hooked on this family. Remember you're free, you're free.' Yet it did not seem to shout so loudly this time.

Back at the motel she thankfully deposited Joshua in his high chair, set out the weetbix, popped the toast in the toaster and plugged in the kettle. She carefully spooned the cereal into the ever-open mouth and then gave them the toast and Marmite while she quickly prepared scrambled eggs and tea for herself and Michelle. She had called Michelle when she came in and was pleased to hear the shower running. That must be a good sign. You don't care about cleanliness if you're going to do yourself in. Michelle must be feeling better.

As she joined them, Shannon was shocked anew at her thinness and the exhaustion on her face, and her almost ethereal beauty.

'I don't know how to thank you.' Michelle put her hand to her mouth, and the tears ran down her cheeks. 'Look, I'm sorry, I cry all the time—I can't seem to help it. Please go on talking as if it wasn't happening.' She kissed both children and sat down. 'I'll just have a cup of tea. I don't feel like eating.'

'Oh no, you don't,' Shannon said firmly. 'I've been out shopping and you just eat up these eggs. No wonder you're weepy if you're not eating!'

She felt quite a bully, yet to her delight Michelle obeyed like a scolded child and silently ate the whole large plateful.

'Thank you again, Shannon.' She looked up with a faint smile. 'You must have had quite a morning.'

As she lifted Joshua down, she noticed Marigold's new top. 'Where did you get that?'

'Shannon bought it, and a new *dress*!' It was a breathless announcement. Marigold rushed for the parcel she had put on the bed. 'Look, it's beautiful!'

'It is indeed.' The tears flowed again. 'I can't pay you—I feel so awful.'

'No need to feel awful,' Shannon informed her. 'I've not had so much fun for ages. That child has an exceptional taste in clothes. She knew exactly what she wanted, and she wasn't rude about it, just firm.'

Michelle was holding the dress. 'Yes, she's always been like that. She'll walk around the materials in a store and she'll touch them so carefully, and she always chooses my clothes for me. That's when I could afford them, before Mark. . . .' Again she turned away.

'Here, I'll pour you a second cup of tea. I could do with one myself.'

Michelle let Marigold outside to play after cautioning her to stay off the street and gave Joshua a battered toy and a couple of pots to play with, before sliding back into her chair. 'I'm so weak, so tired. I lost my pills when I lost my purse . . . I'll have to get some more.'

'We'll go to the doctor. . . .' Shannon began.

'No, not yet. I guess I have to explain a few things to you. You said last night things would look better in the morning, and they do in a way, but the decision I was trying to avoid is still as big, and I still can't make it. If only you'd left me, it would have been all over now.'

Shannon quietly drank her tea. She longed to shout, 'All over for you, but Marigold would have been alone in the world, and it's a rotten world without someone to love you.' Was that Marigold's appeal? Was she feeling again the loss of her father and trying to hold Marigold's world together? No, it was more than that. Nothing could excuse Michelle's taking her own life and Joshua's.

'Look,' Michelle spoke painfully, 'I know you said

you could help, but no one can. You see, the
McCabes are offering to take the two children and
bring them up decently, and Joshua will get Mark's
share of the farm. You see, when Mark went wild
and got into trouble with the law, his father kicked
him out. Then when he married me, his father cut
him out of ever having anything to do with the
property at all. It's a huge place, you know ...
they're big farmers, involved in everything that happens on the Coast. It really hurt Mark, and he just
went on from one thing to the next till he ended up
in jail. It was as if he was driven—to hurt them, to
hurt himself.' She stopped as if remembering the
pain, and her tears flowed unceasingly.

'But do you want hard people like that bringing
up your children?' asked Shannon.

'Not really, but what alternative have I got? I've
made such a mess of it myself. I'm useless. I can't
budget—I can't do anything right. It was all right
when Mark was alive, but I'm hopeless on my own.'

'I think you're crazy talking like that,' Shannon
said fiercely. 'I think you've done wonderfully well
with those children. They're darlings. They're not
neglected. Look at the size of Joshua, nobody could
say he's not well cared for, he's such a contented
baby. And Marigold is really special, she has a tremendous personality, and you've helped develop
that.'

'No, I haven't. You're giving me credit for
something she was born with ... she's like Mark, she
has his assurance, I'm timid and stupid. I'm just a
mess.'

'Rubbish! Marigold has a fantastic faith. You
must have taught her. She's fastidious about her
clothes, that's your training. She's forthright in her
opinions but not rude ... that's your mothering. And
you're not a mess, I think you have a real strength,

but you're just physically run down. Why do you even consider giving them up?'

'Because the Welfare are going to take them off me anyway—they say I'm inadequate. So they go either to strangers or to Mark's family. I have no choice.' Michelle sounded desperate. 'I'm only going to hurt their chances of ever having a decent life if I refuse the McCabes, to grow up in that lovely valley that Mark loved. Oh, I've faced it again and again, and it's the only answer, yet I can't bring myself to hand them over and never see them again. I love them, truly I do!'

'You don't have to convince me,' said Shannon. 'But what have they got against you? They must be monsters . . . trying to separate you from your children.'

Michelle shook her head. 'No, you've got it all wrong. They're good people, well established . . . you know, a bit snooty, but nice. They go to church. . . .'

'Doesn't seem to have done them a lot of good,' Shannon said nastily.

Wearily Michelle brushed away her fair hair. 'Look, you just don't understand. To them my family is just scum. They believe my brothers led Mark astray. Maybe they helped, but he was well on his way before they met up. My brothers *are* a wild lot, always in trouble, always in court, and two of them have been in prison. They're okay when they're sober, but they drink a lot, and when they get drunk they're completely reckless and stupid. Dad never corrected them or disciplined them, and now he can't do anything with them. Mum has always tried, but Dad just yelled her down.'

'You mean they think they're too good for you,' Shannon said savagely. 'Are you like your brothers? Have you been in trouble too?' Somehow it just didn't seem probable.

'No, but I didn't grow up with them. My father only liked boys and he gave me a hard time, and Mum used to send me over to Gran to get me out of the way. Well, in the end I just stayed there. She brought me up from the time I was Marigold's age. Mum used to come and see me sometimes, and even took me home once or twice, but it was no good. Dad seemed to have a set on me, and I was scared of him. The boys were never scared of anything. I suppose that's why he liked them best.'

'So your family wouldn't help you now?' Shannon asked.

'No. Mum would like to, but it's pretty hopeless. She's got enough worries with the boys anyway.'

'But if you had a different upbringing, and Mark's family know that, why are they so hard?' asked Shannon.

'They don't know me personally—they don't want to. You see, we live on the West Coast. It's different from anywhere else in New Zealand. People are closer in a way. But I grew up in Hokitika, and Mark grew up in Inangahua about a hundred miles away. I never met him till after he'd left home. It was about the time Gran died. I was fifteen and went home to live and Mark came in with my brothers and we sort of liked each other, then I got pregnant and we got married. I told you, I'm a mess, I foul up everything.'

'How old were you, Michelle?' Shannon felt like crying with her.

'When I got married? Just sixteen, and Marigold was born that year.'

'How old are you now?'

'I'm twenty.'

'You poor kid! Life hasn't been very fair to you.'

'I married Mark. You can't get much better than that.' Michelle's blue eyes challenged Shannon.

'He was good to you?'

'He was great. He was the greatest. And things were coming right for us too. When he went to his father for help, when I got into trouble, his father was rotten to him, and he seemed to believe all the awful things his father said about him. We moved up North and got in with a really bad lot. Mark just seemed to get worse and worse, trying to prove something ... I don't know what, and they were into drugs, the whole bit, so he ended up in jail too. I was pregnant with Joshua then, but when Mark came out, he'd changed. He got a good job and life was sweet, really sweet—just Mark and me and Marigold. We were so happy. He didn't seem to mind about his family any more.'

She was silent for a long time. 'Well, then I had Josh, and it was a terrible birth, and I took ages to get better, then I got sick a different way ... post-natal depression. Mark took another job as well to pay for me to have someone to help. He did his ordinary work, then came home for a few hours' sleep, and then he'd get up at two and do the milk run. That's how he got killed. He was running delivering the milk and it was foggy, and a car hit him.'

'I'm so sorry, love. He sounds quite a man.'

Michelle sniffed. 'He was ... just wonderful. I was sort of knocked for six, and I didn't claim for benefit straight away, then a clerk mucked it up and I didn't get it for six weeks. I had nothing for the kids, so I took food from a supermarket, and got into arrears with my rent ... oh, you don't want to hear it all. Just that I messed everything up. The Welfare helped me back on my feet twice and I just couldn't seem to cope. Then I had this breakdown and they put the children into care. I told them about Mark's people, the McCabes, and they must have written to them about me. That's when they made the offer. It just about finished me, and no matter how hard I tried, I didn't seem to get any better.'

Shannon was still trying to piece it all together. 'So really Mark's people don't know you at all, or what's been happening to you?'

'Only what the Welfare told them . . . that I was inadequate, which is true. I've proved it—more so now that I escaped from the hospital and picked up the kids without permission. I just fall into one mess after another. I just wanted to hand them over myself, so that I could see where they were to live, and maybe they'd remember later that I didn't want to lose them. But when I picked them up I couldn't go through with it. That's when you came along.'

'I'm glad I came along,' Shannon told her. 'It's about time someone did something for you. Listen carefully. You've been through a terrible time, but you're not inadequate. Anyone would break down after the things you've been through. You just need time to recover. No one could make a wise decision in the state you're in. We'll get in touch with this McCabe lot and tell them you need more time.'

'You can't. They've been only writing through a lawyer. They don't even want to meet me.'

'Rubbish! I won't let them do such a sneaky thing through lawyers. They're going to have to face up to this awful thing they're planning. Where did you say they lived? I don't know the South Island very well. Hang on, I'll get my road map.'

Joshua started to cry, and she picked him up. 'I don't know much about children, Michelle. What's wrong with him?'

A pale smile touched Michelle's lips. 'He's such a good boy. He only cries for three reasons—one, he hates wet pants, two, he's hungry, or three, he's tired. So I guess his pants need changing.'

'Right, Joshua. Dry pants for you!' Shannon

changed him more deftly this time, then found a biscuit in his bag and gave it to him. He smiled immediately, his sunny mood miraculously restored. Shannon brought the map back to the table and found Inangahua Valley halfway down the West Coast side of the Island.

'Well, that's settled. I'll pack the car, and we'll be off. You leave the McCabes to me.'

'The letters only mentioned Mark's older brother James, although he has a sister called Louise,' Michelle told her. 'He won't see you or me—the lawyer was most definite about that.'

'You leave James McCabe to me. It looks like about three hours' drive. Do you think you're up to it? Shouldn't we see a doctor about those pills of yours?'

'No,' Michelle answered stubbornly. 'I want this over. I can't go another day without a decision. Even if I have to give them up it's got to be today. I've got no more steam left. You seem to think you can help, but I know you can't. Look, Mark belonged to them and they cut him off. What makes you think they'll change their ideas for me? It's not on. But because you've been so kind, I give you full control—of me, of the kids. Do your best, but when you fail please don't blame yourself, because I've heard Mark say how strong James is . . . he really admired him. So you've got no show.'

Shannon stood up with her hands on her hips. 'I'm pretty tough too. You'd better watch it, James McCabe, I'm heading your way!' Then her brown eyes lit up and she sang, 'If you see me coming, you'd better step aside, 'cos a lot of men didn't and a lot of men died. Do you remember that song? I'll make it my theme song.'

For a moment something like hope shone in Michelle's extraordinary blue eyes. 'You're so small, yet you think you can beat the world!'

Shannon laughed, 'Sure can. Perhaps not the whole world, but I promise you, even if I lose, James McCabe will know he's been in a fight! But I won't lose. And you promise you'll go to the doctor as soon as we've finished him off.'

Michelle stood up slowly. 'If you can by some miracle, because it will be that, fix it so that I can see my children in the future, I will see a doctor, but if I lose them, what's the point?' She went to her room.

Shannon hastily packed her bits and pieces, paid the motel account and put the children in the car. She pushed away from her mind all the questions that tried to overwhelm her. She would just get them to that town . . . Reefton, see Mighty McCabe, and. . . . Perhaps something would come to her on the drive down. Where was Michelle? She went back into the motel and found her crying on the bed, the half-packed weekend bag beside her. 'I'm sorry, I just haven't enough guts to go on. Take the kids and go.'

'Rubbish! It's not guts you lack, it's physical strength. The faster I get you to the Coast, the faster I get you to a doctor.' Shannon wished she felt as confident as she sounded. Michelle needed a doctor now, but she knew it was useless to argue. She packed the only bag Michelle carried, noting how little it contained. Michelle had only the clothes she stood up in. She put an arm around Michelle and encouraged her out to the car, ran back for the bag and pushed it in the boot.

She drove off, thankful to have accomplished their departure at least. She glanced at the beautiful Picton Harbour with a feeling of regret. She would have loved to spend more time there, but she would come back this way. When she was free again. It was only as that thought penetrated that she admitted she was now very deeply involved, and that her feeling of responsibility was growing each minute. She thrust the thought away.

She saw a petrol station. 'We'll fill up here.' She swung the car in and switched off the engine. Immediately Joshua tried to scramble over the front seat.

'I'll nurse him,' Michelle said in a tired voice, so Shannon lifted him over.

As he grabbed for the steering wheel, she realised her mistake. She prised him loose and he attached himself to the gear lever with a gurgle of satisfaction. Michelle was no match for the energetic baby. Shannon got out to pay the attendant, and suddenly saw a car seat advertisement. Whew!

'Do you sell those things? Do they need a lot of installing?' she asked.

'We've got two styles. One you just clip on. The better model would take us about half an hour.'

'I'll have the clip-on one. We're in a hurry. I have to get to the West Coast as fast as I can.'

He brought a lovely padded car seat out and fitted it on to the back seat. 'There you are! Hey, young fellow, try it out for size.' He caught Joshua by surprise, lifted him from his mother's knee in one swift movement and settled him in the chair. Joshua chuckled and grabbed a handful of his hair, and by the time he had laughingly extricated himself, Joshua was imprisoned.

Shannon was full of admiration. 'You've obviously got children yourself. Would you like a trip to the Coast with us?'

'I wouldn't mind.' His eyes took in her trim figure and sparkling brown eyes. 'I think my wife might be a bit put out. You'll be taking the Tophouse route, of course?'

'The what?'

'Tophouse. It'll cut an hour off your journey. Here, get your map and I'll show you. There's no need to go away over to Nelson, you cut through along the Waiau. You'll enjoy it.'

Shannon paid him by cheque, and expressed her very real thanks for the short-cut he'd shown her. She wondered how Joshua would take to being restricted, but he settled down happily. He could now see out of the window, and whenever he managed to catch sight of Shannon's eyes in the rear vision mirror his grin broadened and his eyes shone. Golly, she was so lucky to have such a happy baby! It was clear by the way Michelle had sagged back in the seat that she was going to be beyond offering any help.

The miles flew by, and Marigold chattered away to Joshua, to Shannon, to her mother, and quite frequently to herself. Michelle was genuinely worried about all the money Shannon was spending on them, but admitted the car seat was essential.

'Forget it. I've got plenty, and I can sell it again.' Shannon had thought she had plenty of money when she left home, but then she had only been counting on keeping herself. She had saved for five years, waiting for this time when she could start her own life. Her only extravagance had been this little old Humber, named lovingly the Yellow Peril by the girls. It did not look beautiful, but it had never let her down and she was completely satisfied with it. Shannon had felt not a twinge of envy or embarrassment as she had parked in the drive by the variety of elegant and expensive cars of William and the young men who had moved in a never-ending line in and out the girls' lives. Even Simon with his fabulous Ferrari had grown to have a reluctant admiration for the performance of her darling Yellow Peril.

As she drove, thoughts floated in and out of her mind, and she knew that her problems were blotting out appreciation of the fantastic countryside and scenery. She sighed. She would repeat this trip again with more time to enjoy it . . . when she was on her own again. Her father had said 'Run before the wind', but at the moment she felt she was being caught in the fringe of a hurricane, and knew that when she met James McCabe this afternoon, it would be blowing in full force.

All she really wanted was to make him accept the fact that Michelle needed her children and they needed her, that if he was going to take control of the children he had to leave room in the plan for their mother. If she failed to make him accept that, then she had to get time, to postpone the decision until Michelle was fit enough to make a wise choice. Surely that was not too much to ask?

But say he did agree? What then? Michelle was very sick. Even if she got a month or six weeks' grace, who would care for the children? Who would support and encourage Michelle? Even as she faced the thought she tried to twist away from the answer. There was no one but herself. If she abandoned them now, there was no prospect of her driving off blithely and enjoying her trip, her freedom. For ever she would be haunted by the knowledge that she had been an instrument in saving Michelle from taking her own life and Joshua's, and then, after buoying her up with a day and night of hope, callously left them to make it on their own. She couldn't do it. Always she would wonder if they had made it. Worse, she would be carrying with her the idea that her own stubborn, selfish desire to be free had meant more to her than someone else's suffering.

Shannon took a deep breath. What did it matter if she committed herself to a month, or six weeks?

And if she did, how long would her money last? She had saved enough to have a leisurely six weeks around the South Island, with enough left over for a flight to England, and a little over to keep her a couple of months. It had seemed a lot of money yesterday. After paying for the motel and food, Marigold's clothes, the car seat, she knew it would melt away like snow.

For sure Michelle would be entitled to Welfare Benefit, but maybe they wouldn't pay it, if she had run away from the hospital and taken back the care of the children? Well, say it cost her a thousand dollars. It wouldn't kill her to take another job and save up again. No, it wouldn't, but she resented the idea of the time it would take. She was free and running, and would have to tie herself to some dull routine for ages.

Oh, she was being stupid, trying to cross too many bridges before she came to them. Why, these McCabes might accept their responsibility without question. They had never met Michelle. Once they talked with her, they would know their assumptions were all wrong. It was simply a matter of being firm and resolute, discussing it in a calm and unemotional meeting. Her spirits started to lift. She would take a motel room in Reefton—she had to have a base— and ring up Mighty McCabe and tell him to get himself in there and make him see he was behaving irresponsibly and irrationally. Nothing to it. She'd be on her way tomorrow with the wee family left secure and protected.

Joshua was grizzling, and struggling to get out of his seat. Shannon glanced at Michelle, who had fallen asleep. Her pale face and dark shadowed eyes told Shannon she was on her own. What had Michelle said this morning? If he cries, he's got wet pants, or he's hungry, or he's sleepy. Which one?

'Hey, Marigold, have you got any of those jelly-beans left?' she asked.

'No. I ate them all.'

'Silly question. What will we feed Joshua? Any ideas?'

'Mummy gives him a bottle sometimes when she puts him down.'

'Good thinking, except I haven't got any milk. We'll stop if we see a shop. There should be a country store along here somewhere. Play with him. Give him my torch, it's up the back window. Switch it on and off to keep him happy.'

Marigold scrambled up to obey, and again Shannon felt love flow towards the little girl. Her ruse worked and she heard Joshua chuckling with pleasure at the game. Thankfully she saw a small township ahead. She pulled in by the store and got both children out, then remembered the bottle was in the bag in the boot. Joshua was not amused, and she observed there was nothing wrong with the condition of his lungs, as she struggled to hold him and extract the bottle.

She bought milk, and the shopkeeper filled the bottle for her, and she noticed Marigold fingering a book on the display stand. She would need something to amuse her for the rest of the trip.

'Take two or three, Marigold. I'll read them to you tonight, and I'll get some biscuits, too, and a fizzy drink for you. I'd rather not stop for a meal. Anything else?'

'Mummy sometimes gets those little cheese things and an orange for us.'

'You're a treasure.' Hastily Shannon added the cheese segments and fruit to her order, then carried them back to the car. 'I'll change his pants and lie him on the seat, and he might sleep. You won't have much room, love.'

'I don't mind,' Marigold said obligingly. 'Do you think I could try Joshua's chair? Would it break?'

'I don't think so. You're a lot taller than bouncer here, but you're very light. Hop in and we'll see.'

Marigold settled herself quite comfortably, and began to enjoy her books. Shannon changed Joshua and pulled his trousers on again, while he blissfully sucked his bottle, his eyelids falling shut. As she drove off she was delighted to hear Marigold announce. 'He's gone to sleep.'

The rest of the trip was far more peaceful than Shannon could have imagined. Joshua and Michelle slept, and Marigold kept her informed about the pictures in the book while Shannon made up stories to fit them. It was a real relief to drive into the small town of Reefton not much after three o'clock. She found a motel, and with Marigold at her heels booked them in. She transferred the luggage inside before waking Michelle and Joshua.

Michelle seemed so much weaker, unable to stand or walk on her own, and Shannon's heart quaked. Had she done the right thing, dragging her two hundred miles before getting medical attention? Michelle seemed in a daze, beyond caring. There was no way she would be able to talk to the McCabes.

As she clung to Shannon, Michelle looked around her. 'This is a pretty place. Look at the river. And see up on the hill above the town, there's a big white cross. We'll be all right here.'

Shannon followed her gaze, and saw on the golden gorse-covered hillside a large white-painted wooden cross near the top. 'Hope you're right.' Her voice didn't carry a lot of conviction. She helped Michelle into bed and then went back to get the protesting Joshua. As she picked him out he grabbed her hair and pulled her face down to deliver a moist kiss.

Shannon hugged him. 'You're a wee beaut! That sleep has put you in a good mood. That makes one of us. I'm exhausted and the worst is yet to come. We'll have to find a phone and make contact with the enemy.'

'Who's the enemy?' Marigold asked, her blue eyes bright with interest.

'Well, I'm not sure . . . yet!' Shannon realised she would have to be more careful over her choice of words. Marigold might yet be living with the McCabes by evening. There was no use putting her against them.

'Could I have a bath and put on my new dress?' Marigold asked hopefully.

'I think that's a fantastic idea.' She carried Joshua into the lounge and checked that it was safe as he crawled off on a journey of exploration. 'Could you keep an eye on him while I make a phone call? I won't be long.'

'I'm tired,' Marigold protested.

'I'm sure you are, you've had a long trip and you've been so good. I won't be long, I promise. Then you'll have a bath, and put on your pretty dress. Perhaps you would like a sleep after that.'

'I never sleep in the daytimes,' Marigold said firmly. Then after a moment, 'Unless I'm very, very tired.'

'You think about it, while I'm ringing up.'

Shannon went to the phone, determined to get it over with. She checked the name, found the number, and then the enormity of what she was trying to do hit her. Her mouth went dry, her confidence drained away. She had no idea of how to coerce this McCabe man into any sort of a compromise. She was actually violating one of her most cherished principles. She had lived by the code of not interfering in people's lives; she had no experience in manipulating and swaying people to change of heart or direction. Yet she had to try. What if he just hung up? Should she be pleasant but firm, should she be icily polite, should she try for the goodhumoured but sensible touch? She must have been mad to get herself into this. Should she try a frantic call to Simon in Wellington? He was a lawyer, he could advise her. She tried to imagine the conversation with him, and threw the whole idea away. He would be devastating in his condemnation . . . she knew it. If she could not even discuss it with Simon who was a friend, how did she know how to persuade this McCabe, who according to Michelle had all the softness of the Rock of Gibraltar, that she had any business or authority to alter things?

Resolutely she dialled the number and as the buzz-buzz sounded at the other end, she hoped he would be out. She would have time before she had to ring back, to quell the rising fears and nausea. If he was out she would just leave a message.

'James McCabe speaking.' He had a firm assured voice.

Hoping the wires would not carry the wobble in her voice, Shannon said, 'Shannon Haldane here. I'm staying at the Bluebird Motel in Reefton. I've just booked in, and I have something very important I wish to discuss with you. Could you please give me half an hour of your time?'

'Who are you?' His voice crackled with authority. 'What's your business?'

She felt like telling him she was an insurance agent and hanging up. Keep cool. 'I have your niece and nephew with me, Joshua and Marigold McCabe. I want to discuss their future with you.'

There was a significant silence. 'Miss Haldane, 'I'll give you my lawyer's telephone number and I advise you to contact him. He'll deal with any problem you may have.'

'I will not speak to your lawyer! Unless you come in personally and discuss the situation you can forget that these children exist, and I'll make other arrangements for their future. Goodbye.' She hung up, and felt her knees turn to water. She could hardly stand. If he had that effect on her over the phone, what would it be like meeting him face to face? Would he even bother to come? He might just ignore her. What would she do then? Damn James McCabe!

CHAPTER THREE

SHANNON returned to the motel and dragged Joshua from under the settee where he had become securely wedged, pacified him with an orange, and turned on the bath for Marigold. She tried to marshal her thoughts into some sort of order. James McCabe could walk in at any moment, but her mind remained a total blank. She must be suffering from delayed shock. He had sounded so sure of himself. What could she say to convince him? No answer came.

Joshua joined them and insisted on joining Marigold in the bath. That kept her too occupied to spare any further thoughts to a solution. By the time she had dressed them both, she was drained and only wished she could join Michelle for a sleep. Looking after children was not for the inactive, incapable, and unfit.

'You look beautiful, Marigold,' Shannon said as the little girl paraded in her pretty new dress. 'The colour just matches your eyes.'

'Can I see myself in the mirror?'

'You surely can! You're a real picture.' She took her through to the other bedroom. If her uncle wasn't pleased with his niece, he'd be a hard man to please. Marigold's fair hair was neatly brushed and her small face was flushed with pleasure.

'I'm beautiful,' Marigold announced without a trace of conceit. 'Can I show Mummy?'

'No, love—Mummy's asleep. We'll have to wait till she wakes up. Are you still tired? Would you like to pop into this nice bed for a nap? I'll wake you as soon as Mummy gets up.' If there was going to be a nasty scene she preferred Marigold not to witness it.

'I might,' Marigold considered the proposal seriously. 'Yes, I will, then I can stay up later tonight, can't I?'

'Yes, love.' Shannon tried not to show her anxiety. Where would Marigold be tonight? She was so happy, so unconscious of the fact that she might never see her mother again after tonight. Fiercely Shannon rejected the thought, as she took off the dress and tucked Marigold under the covers.

'I'll have to close the door or else Joshua will crawl in here, but I'll just be next door. Just call out when you've had your sleep.'

'Could I have my books, please?'

'Aren't I silly not to have thought of that!' Shannon hurried out and returned with them. She hugged Marigold quickly and went out, fighting back an urge to cry. Children of that age usually had a heap of treasured and well battered toys. That child had nothing from her past except the memory of her father, and this man McCabe was ready to take even her mother.

She put the kettle on, realising she had not had lunch herself. She peeled an orange while it boiled, laughing as Joshua crawled swiftly over and hauled himself up against her knee with a look of happy anticipation. Should she change? Would she make a better impression in a dress? Swiftly she pulled out her case and selected an attractive green suede dress and put on stockings and high-heeled shoes, before renewing her make-up. The tension was building up in her . . . would he come? Or would he stay away? Which was worse? She should have set a time, that would have been more professional. Professional what? She giggled a little hysterically. She could only be described as unskilled labour in the forthcoming struggle!

The kettle boiled and she made the tea and poured it. No negative thinking, now, she admonished herself, no emotion either. Men were not impressed by emotional and passionate arguments. She had to be quite cool, determined and passionate, and present the facts rationally. She heard a vehicle drive up and brake violently outside the reception area. Seconds later a Land Rover stopped outside the window, and out of it stepped a tall lean muscular man, with thick dark wavy hair, dressed in checked shirt and jeans. He was over six feet tall, maybe six foot four. Oh, she was glad she had on her high-heeled shoes . . . and that she'd changed. By the look on that angry handsome face she was going to need all the odds she could muster on her side.

She had no doubt she was seeing James McCabe. Whew! When the sharp knock came at the door, even though she had been prepared for it, her hand shook so badly that the cup rattled on the saucer, and tea slopped all over the place.

She walked quickly to the door. 'Mr McCabe—so glad you could come in. Would you like a cup of tea?' She didn't give him time to answer but turned her back and walked back to the table. She had to get him inside; it was too easy for him to stride away from the step.

'This is not a social visit, so we'll dispense with tea.'

She looked up then, and sighed with relief. He was inside, and Joshua was crawling rapidly towards him. 'Please close the door or Joshua will escape.' She poured herself another cup of tea, not because she wanted it, but it kept her from meeting his eyes. Thankfully she heard the door close. At least she'd got this far safely. The glimpse she had had through the window had told her that keeping control of the conversation would not be easy.

'If you would take a seat, I'd like to explain my phone call,' she went on.

'I'd prefer to stand.'

'I would prefer it if you would sit down. This is not easy for me to explain, and I would like to conduct this conversation in a civilised manner if possible.' She looked at him directly for the first time, and her heart sank. He was mad all right—fighting mad! But to her surprise he strode towards the table and sat down. It didn't make him appear any less formidable.

'Who are you, Miss Haldane?' he demanded. 'Are you from the Welfare Department? I gave explicit instructions that all dealings were to be through my lawyer. I'm justifiably annoyed to find that those instructions have been disregarded, and I'm awaiting your explanation.'

Shannon smiled at him. Her slightly crooked grin held unexpected appeal, and amusement showed in her brown eyes. She was sure it wasn't often anyone disregarded *his* instructions. This was going to be a whole new experience for him. Some of her fear left her. It was like jumping in at the deep end of the swimming pool, once in the water there were only two options . . . sink or swim, and she had to swim.

'I'm waiting, Miss Haldane.'

'Yes, I know, and it's extremely good of you.' She gave him another warm smile. 'This is a very tricky situation, and I'm trying to present it to you in the best possible light.'

'Are you from the Welfare Department?'

For a moment she was sorely tempted to say she was, to claim the protection of a large government department, but she met his steel blue gaze steadily. 'No, I'm not with the Government.'

Joshua had made the round trip and was now at

James McCabe's feet. Grunting and puffing with determination, he pulled himself to his feet. Using his uncle's jeans as a help, he finally made it upright and beamed with love at the dark angry man.

'Well, who the hell *are* you?'

He kept his eyes on Shannon. She realised that he would have jumped to his feet, except that he suddenly became aware of Joshua. 'Aren't you going to acknowledge your nephew's greetings?' she asked accusingly.

He glared at her. 'Answer my question!' Then, almost against his will, he turned towards the baby, and Joshua reached up confidently to be lifted up. The man hesitated, but just as Joshua overbalanced, he reached out and lifted him on to his knee. Joshua's smile of triumph was a thing of pure beauty and love.

Shannon watched the incredible change sweep over the man's face as he stared at the boy. It was a look of intense pain and grief, so intense that Shannon turned away, not willing to witness such hurt. Yet even as she turned she saw the longing and loneliness in his eyes.

'Dear God, he's the image of Mark! My young brother, Mark. He was killed ... but you'd know that. ...' He seemed to be talking to himself. His strong brown hand gently stroked Joshua's golden baby hair, and the baby chuckled responsively, then crowed with delight at all the attention he was getting, before turning to grab the packet of biscuits which were now within reach of his always exploring hands.

James McCabe placed him carefully on the floor, and Shannon said a little huskily, 'You can give him a biscuit. It will keep him quiet.'

As he handed Joshua the biscuit and turned towards Shannon the hard grim expression was back in place, and she quickly forestalled his question.

'I'm a friend of Michelle, Mark's wife. As you would know from the Welfare, she hasn't been well. In fact she's seriously ill and in no condition to make any sort of decision, certainly not one which will have such lasting consequences. The pressure that's been put on her to choose either to let the children go to you, and probably never see them again. . . .'

'Not probably, Miss Haldane, definitely never see them again. That was made quite clear by my lawyer.'

'But why, Mr McCabe? Could you please explain to me the reason behind this insistence, so that I can understand it?'

'No. What authority do you have to ask me to explain my motives? They satisfy me.'

'I would be grateful if you would explain them so they would satisfy me too.'

'Why should I?' He was arrogantly sure of himself.

'Because at the moment I'm in control of these children. Their mother has handed the whole responsibility over to me. She's too ill to fight for her rights.'

'She has no rights. She has proved that. She's totally incompetent, she's been in debt, she's been evicted from her flat for not paying her rent, she was found ill and sharing a squatters' flat with some thoroughly disreputable people, the children were being neglected. She was caught shoplifting. The Welfare people have propped her up again and again, and have finally decided she'll never be able to care for them. They got in touch with me, and I made my offer. I will not have a person of her background involved in their upbringing.'

Shannon felt her control slipping, but held her anger. 'She's their mother. What other woman could care for them as lovingly?'

'None, because the question doesn't arise. They'll be brought up without a woman to undermine any training I give them.'

Shannon gasped. 'You haven't got anyone to care for them at all?'

James McCabe returned her scrutiny without flinching. 'I didn't say that. I said no woman. There are perfectly good male nurses about ... for that matter male teachers, even kindergarten teachers. Many solo parents are male. Women have not got the sole prerogative of rearing children.'

Shannon stared at him appalled. 'That's monstrous! Children need the softening influence of a woman in their lives, especially at this very impressionable infant stage.' She stood up angrily and walked over and picked Joshua up and cuddled him. James McCabe couldn't mean what he said—but one look at that implacable expression and jutting chin and she knew that he did. She had better try something else. It would not be possible to reach a compromise on that question.

'You say Michelle has an unfortunate background. . . .'

'That's a flattering description of her family. They're well known for their shiftless, irresponsible, criminal behaviour. If I took the children I would make sure they were never in contact with that brood, you can be sure of that.'

'You've never met Michelle,' she protested. 'How dare you condemn her out of hand?'

His blue eyes were flint. 'I don't have to meet her. I have her history from the Welfare, and it makes very sorry reading. If I wanted more, I wouldn't have to travel far. This is the Coast. There's one newspaper to cover the whole sparsely populated area, so all news is published in it, and her family have featured prominently with convincing frequency for years. I dare to criticise her, because she deserves nothing but that.'

'You know nothing about her at all!' Shannon shouted. 'Just what you've read in the paper and what some over-officious public servant has written. How would you like to be judged on such evidence?'

'Feel completely free to judge me by anything you can find in the local papers, Miss Haldane.' His smile was as sarcastic as his voice.

'Listen—Michelle doesn't really belong to that family. She was brought up by her grandmother. She's a fine person, really she is. Won't you please meet her, speak with her, make your own decision on her character?' Shannon was pleading now. She had never met anyone so iron-hard as this man—rock-solid, confirmed in his own opinion. Why had she thought she could change him?

'I have no need to meet her. Tell me, how long have you known her?'

Shannon bit her lip, but could not lie. 'I met her last night on the ferry.'

He laughed derisively. 'And on that short acquaintance, you've put aside several competent professional opinions. You have the unmitigated nerve to set yourself up as an expert on a five-minute acquaintance! What right have you to become involved?'

'Have you no understanding or compassion? Why don't you listen to me? You sit there secure in your arrogance and wealth and property, and you're putting down a girl who never had a chance. Look at Joshua—can you describe him as neglected?'

'Of course not! Because he's been in care for the last month. Your argument defeats itself. And I have compassion and understanding for the children—something you seem to be overlooking. I want to give them a secure and comfortable home. They're my brother's children. I want to give them all they're entitled to ... and that doesn't include a prison record by the time they're in their teens. Is there anything wrong with that? State your objections.'

She had none. He had everything to offer Marigold and Joshua. But there had to be room for Michelle. 'I think that's very good. You're offering a great deal. Couldn't you be even more generous, and include Mark's young wife in that kindness too? If you'd offered any suport at all when your brother died, she would never have come to this low point.'

James McCabe stood up. 'You don't know what you're asking. It was because of her that we lost all contact with Mark. Because of that little slut my father kicked him out and cut him from his will. We could have mended our fences, but she trapped him with a pregnancy. Her family dragged Mark into their orbit, and dragged him down with them, and you ask me to help her? I suppose she's appealed to your sympathy and twisted all the facts so you see us as the oppressors. . . . Grow up!'

White-faced, her brown eyes enormous with anger, Shannon turned on him. 'No! That's why I know you're wrong and I'm right. You, from your high-and-mighty position, have done nothing but throw accusations and slander at a young sick girl, but she's done the very opposite. In spite of the very ugly thing your family are trying to do to her, she has said nothing unkind about you. She even tried to explain to me your attitude and how you meant it for the best. She said you were church people—huh! She's been sharing *your* burden. Who supported and loved and helped your brother back on his feet? She did. Where were you when he was in jail? Visiting him? No. You were too busy protecting your position and your respectable name.'

Shannon fought back her tears.

'She's lying there in the room next to you. I think she's dying. She has nothing to live for now Mark has gone, nothing except the children, and you're taking them! I only wanted to ask you to give her a few more weeks to decide whether to give them to you or not. Just let her get on her feet and see if she can cope. I'll stay with her. Please can't you even offer that much?'

'No, I can't. Say she did come right, how long would she last on her own? I've seen it again and again, and if you're honest you'll agree with me. People repeat their errors. She'll hang on for a bit, then marry someone else, and have more children. What will happen to Marigold and Joshua then? A stepfather who resents them? Beats them? Teaches them to rob and steal and flout the law? Are you prepared to be responsibile for them having to grow up in that sort of atmosphere? Don't rush in. Think about it. It's not only possible, you'll agree, but entirely probable.'

Shannon felt her heart sink. What he was saying was entirely true. It could happen. It wasn't a certainty, as he was implying, but it could happen. And she would be solely responsible for it. James McCabe had everything to offer—a good family name, respectability, an inheritance, a childhood growing up on a farm, first class education at the best schools. . . . Now she knew why Michelle had even contemplated giving them up. And Michelle had found it too much to decide, and had given the decision to her. Had she the right to deny the children these things?

As if sensing victory James McCabe did not push her. He just waited . . . waited for her to acknowledge that he was right. It was worse than when he was speaking . . . then she had responded automatically.

'What have you got to offer?' he demanded as if sure of the answer.

That did it. She had no choice. 'A chance for Michelle to live. You haven't asked where I met her or how. You haven't cared. Well, she was preparing to jump overboard on the ferry, to take her own life. And she was taking Joshua with her, because she couldn't bear to give him up. I saved him first and then her, so in a way I'm responsible for their being alive at this minute.'

She kissed Joshua, hiding her face in his baby softness. 'He wouldn't even be here for you to offer anything if I hadn't been there. Even if you're right, and I'm not saying you are, I can't make a decision that will kill Michelle. She's lying there next door. She wouldn't even see a doctor until I'd spoken to you. If I agree to your having the children, she'll refuse to get medical help, and that's the same as if I'd murdered her. She trusts me. You've rubbished her—well, you can keep all your professional opinions. I know she's decent, and she's just knocked about by the load she's carried, a load your so smug and self-satisfied family have stood back and let her carry almost to her grave . . . waiting like vultures to get your hands on her only treasure!'

Shannon thrust the startled Joshua into his arms. 'Cuddle him now, because you'll never get your hands on him again. You talk about your wonderful family and its land and connections. You keep them! You call her family scum, you call her a slut, yet she has more to offer than money. People in glasshouses shouldn't throw stones. If Joshua has the choice between turning out like Michelle or you, I know which I'd choose for him. You lot threw Mark out, and then to absolve yourselves from blame, Michelle was made the scapegoat. But he was a fine boy and a loving father, and I'll see his children don't grow up in the same heartless, sterile home that fostered you. You're a heartless, cruel wretch, who would let her die. . . . I can't bear to even breathe the same air as you!'

She ran from the room, tears streaming down her cheeks, and slamming the door behind her headed towards the bridge. She laid her hot wet cheeks against the cool balustrade, not trying to hold back the sobs that shook her. She'd blown the whole thing. She was ashamed of the awful words she had spoken, deeply ashamed. She had never been so rude and ugly to another human being. She had wanted to hit him, to pound some feeling into him, and she had never felt violent before in her life. It made her sick—not at him; at herself. Slowly she pulled herself together and made her way to the small patch of lawn bordered with brilliant coloured flowers in front of the motel. The Land Rover was still parked there, so she sat down on the grass to think of what came next. What a mess!

As soon as James McCabe left, she would ring a doctor. Michelle was in urgent need of attention. Then she would rent a house for them; no matter how long it took she would support and care for them. She knuckled her eyes. No matter what he said about Michelle making a disastrous marriage, Shannon had more faith in Michelle's judgment. She had chosen Mark. She would choose well the second time, as long as she was given time to get on her feet. She would always put her children first; Shannon didn't know how she knew, but deep within her heart she knew.

She had taken on a huge commitment, and it scared her. She could forget about a life of her own, for a long time . . . maybe years. How Simon would laugh! He had read her character correctly. She had been wrong. It didn't give her a great deal of confidence in herself.

A shadow came between her and the sun, and she looked up to see James McCabe standing over her with Joshua asleep in his arms. She tried to wipe her tearstained face. She would have to apologise.

'There's a little girl in a blue dress inside asking for you.' His expression was enigmatic. 'I have to go home, but I'll be back in half an hour. I'll send the doctor round immediately. Here, take Joshua.'

Shannon sniffed and scrambled to her feet, staring at him in open-mouthed amazement, as she took Joshua into her arms.

'You wanted six weeks for Mark's wife to get well and make an unpressured decision. Well, I accede to your request, but there are conditions. You will take care of the children, but you will live at the farm. I'll take care of all the financial details, for her medical bills, for clothing, feeding, etc., for the three of them, and you will receive a wage for your services. Do you accept?'

'I don't want any money for what I do!' Her heart was lifting. She had not blown it all. The children might still have the best possible life, *and their mother*. Her eyes were shining, then she became nervous. What had changed his mind?

'You take it or leave it, as I offered it.'

She capitulated hastily. She could not jeopardise the children's chances for her own pride's sake. 'Right, I accept. Why are you doing this?'

'Not to gain your respect or goodwill,' he answered savagely. 'I'll be back by the time the doctor arrives. You've been criminally negligent to let that girl get into such a condition without seeking medical help!'

He strode away and climbed into the Land Rover, driving off without a parting glance at Shannon. She glared speechlessly after him. He was trying to put all the blame on her. She was glad she'd been rude to him. If she had to live in the same house as him for six weeks she would probably be rude again. *Arrogant beast!* She headed for the motel.

She saw Marigold as she entered, her blue dress on back to front, and her small face flushed and indignant. Michelle was lying on the settee with her eyes closed, but the tears were sliding down to wet her hair.

'What's happened, Marigold?' Shannon put the sleeping boy beside his mother.

'That man spoiled my dress—that big man. I told him, but he wouldn't listen.'

'I know the feeling. He's naughty not to listen. Come on, I'll put it on properly. Men don't know anything about clothes.'

As she helped Marigold to change the dress a small muffled voice accused, 'You *said* you'd be here when I called. And I called and called, and then I cried.'

Shannon cuddled her. 'I'm sorry, Marigold, truly I am. That was bad of me to do such a thing. Will you forgive me? I just went outside for a minute.'

'Was a long time,' said Marigold, a little mollified. 'And Mummy heard me crying and tried to come and get me, and then when she opened the door she just fell over. That man, that big man, he came and picked her up and put her on the sofa. He was crabby.'

'He sure was,' Shannon agreed with a chuckle. She must be crazy to be laughing when Michelle was so ill, but the thought of James McCabe trying to cope with Joshua asleep, Michelle fainting, and Marigold trying to get into her dress was too delicious not to get some amusement from it all. Serve him right, looking all smug and self-righteous. Golly, she was tired! Was it only yesterday that she had been bridesmaid at the wedding? Life had seemed so simple.

'Are you all right, Michelle?' Shannon asked.

'Yes. Can I have a cup of tea, please?'

'Sure.' Again she plugged in the kettle. 'I haven't got much to eat here, and I don't like to leave you with the children. There's oranges, biscuits and cheese.'

'I don't feel like eating, just a drink, please.'

When Shannon took the tea over, she was shocked to find Michelle could not even sit up properly. She put her arm around her for support.

'Did you see James McCabe?' she asked.

Michelle sipped her tea. 'No. Was he here? What did he say?'

Shannon was surprised at her lack of interest, almost as if his visit had no connection with her. 'He said he'll let you get well before you have to decide about the children. And I'm allowed to take care of them for you.'

'That's nice,' Michelle answered in the same tired voice. 'I don't want any more.' She slid back on the settee and closed her eyes.

Shannon sighed, then feeling Michelle's cold hand brought a blanket through from the bedroom, and tucked it around her.

Marigold and Joshua were crawling in and out the rooms playing a game, so she quickly poured herself a cup of fresh tea and took a biscuit. It was stupid to feel so shaky, but the strain of caring for this family and their problems had exhausted her. She hated to admit it, but it was a relief to have James McCabe on the scene taking control. She would never tell him so, of course, but the sheer strength and size of him was reassuring. She had no doubt that he would make all the decisions when he came back, and she would let him, unless they were against the children's best interests. She had gained her victory . . . time, so now she could relax a little.

She wished the doctor would come, then they could get pills for Michelle and take her to the farm to get well. Six weeks relaxing on a farm in the fresh country air would put new heart in her. Shannon would do all the work with the children, and she was sure that after having Michelle and the children together on the farm for that time, James McCabe would know he couldn't separate them.

She propped her face wearily on her hands. She was so overwhelmingly relieved at the way things had worked out. It would not be easy, living in the same house as that supercilious, domineering McCabe, but it was only for a few weeks. She'd have Michelle with her. Then a thought struck her. Was he married? Who else lived on the farm? No, he couldn't be married; he had said there would be no females around. How could she have forgotten that? The original chauvinist pig! But she must not let her antagonism towards him affect the children—after all, they *had* to like him.

Idly she wondered what had changed his mind. He had done a complete volte-face. She jerked upright and stared at Michelle as the awful suspicion flooded her mind. James McCabe thought Michelle was going to die or be committed to an institution for life. It was the only explanation. She looked at the painfully thin, beautiful girl lying on the settee, and fear clutched her heart. What if Michelle didn't make it? What then? He would have the children already established under his care and protection. Oh, she wished she had not rushed so quickly to accept his offer. It would have been much better to have taken a house and kept them all away from him.

There was knock at the door, and Shannon walked towards it, just as a huge sleek-lined station wagon drew up outside. As she opened the door to a pleas-

ant fair-haired young man, James McCabe stepped
out of the station wagon. He had changed his
clothes as well as his vehicle and was immaculate in
a well cut suit and elegant shirt and matching tie,
and he strode towards them with a firm purposeful
step.

'Glad you could make it so fast, Brad. I'm very
concerned about my sister-in-law's state of health.'
Then with a casual hand, he indicated Shannon.
'This is Dr Clark, Miss Haldane. She's been taking
care of Michelle. Come in, Brad.'

Shannon glared as he brushed past her in the
doorway. In one clever move he had taken full control, relegating her to some sort of home help with
no say in the discussion. Well, she certainly was not
going to let him get away with it!

She smiled warmly at the young man. 'Yes, please
do come in, Dr Clark. I'm a friend of Michelle's and
have travelled with her from Wellington. She's been
under a great deal of stress. These are her children,
Marigold and Joshua McCabe. I wanted to take her
to a doctor in Picton this morning, but there was
some urgent family business requiring her attention
here today, so she insisted on travelling.'

'Good. Thank you, Miss Haldane. I'll just take a
look at her now and will probably need to ask you a
few questions later.'

Shannon flicked a smouldering glance at James,
then grinned. She had wiped out his initial advan-
tage and established her own position.

Joshua had claimed James as a long-lost friend
and was making irresistible advances, and Shannon
saw the stern face soften incredibly as the tall man
bent to pick him up. Marigold stood back, her scowl
showing she had not forgotten the incident with her
best dress.

'I think if you take the children for a walk, Miss

Haldane, the doctor would be able to examine his patient in a quieter atmosphere.'

Shannon's brown eyes narrowed dangerously. 'I don't trust you, James McCabe, and I don't think Michelle has any reason to either. This deep concern you're showing for her has been of very short duration. You may be her brother-in-law, and the doctor may be a friend of yours, but I have the say as to what happens to Michelle and the children, so don't think you can pull rank and send me from the room.'

'You do have a suspicious mind, Miss Haldane! I hardly think Dr Clark will be impressed by your lack of faith in his integrity,' James said smoothly. 'But apart from the fact that he's my friend, you'll have to abide by his diagnosis, because he's the only doctor in Reefton.'

Shannon stiffened. James McCabe had won that round by making the doctor annoyed with her. Nevertheless, she stood her ground and waited.

At last the doctor turned away from Michelle. 'Now, James, you described what you think is the cause of this illness when you rang me. Have you the papers from the Welfare people with you?' He accepted the letters and glanced quickly through them, glanced at the children, then re-read them.

He turned and smiled at Shannon. 'Now, Miss Haldane, would you tell me all you know about Mrs McCabe?'

'She only met her last night,' James said significantly.

'Go ahead, Miss Haldane, take your time. You won't be interrupted.'

Relieved that the doctor was not taking sides, Shannon quickly and concisely told him all she knew.

Dr Clark nodded his head. 'Well, so far, so good.

You gave me the name of the hospital Mrs McCabe left, and as she was only a voluntary patient there's been no harm done, except for the fact that she lost her tablets and has been without them for a whole day. They gave her medical history—and now I'd like to talk to her alone. Would you please both step outside?'

His tone brooked no argument, and after a moment's hesitation Shannon walked out with Marigold by the hand, closely followed by James carrying Joshua. They did not speak and the tension between them was indescribable. Both children rolled on the grass in the sunshine, completely unaware that the two adults were behaving like two sparring animals warily circling, waiting for the opportunity to close for the kill. From the road they probably looked like a very attractive family group, a handsome distinguished father, a dainty adorable mother, and two sweet children.

At last the door opened and Dr Clark beckoned them inside. After cautioning Marigold not to go on the street, Shannon picked Joshua up and walked into the motel. The serious expression on the young doctor's face made her heart pound. What would be his verdict? She glanced at Michelle, but there was no help there. She seemed to be sleeping peacefully.

'Well, I've talked with Michelle, and she has agreed with me to re-enter hospital until her treatment is complete. I've explained to her there's a very good psychiatric hospital in Hokitika, and she's quite happy to be admitted there. Her mind is at rest about the children—she stipulated that Miss Haldane has total authority over them. Now about the arrangements . . .'

Shannon's eyes filled with tears. 'How ill is she, Dr Clark? Will she . . . will she get better?'

'Certainly.' His smile was very pleasant and reassuring. 'She may be there, say, two weeks or four weeks, and if she has the farm to convalesce at, she'll be on her feet in no time. I think I could best describe her present situation by saying she's been under stress for far too long, and is like a torch which has been left on till the batteries run flat and there's very little light left. Well, her batteries are flat, but they'll recharge, with care and rest and a good diet. Now shall I send her down in the ambulance, or would you rather take her, James? To be honest, she'd be more comfortable in a private car.'

'I'll take her, Brad. It's only an hour and a half down there. Is she ready now?'

'Yes. I won't give her any medication—they'll fix her up when she arrives.' He turned to Shannon. 'Stop worrying. It's an excellent hospital and the staff have a fine reputation.'

'Are you sure she understood about the children?' asked Shannon anxiously. 'She didn't seem to take it in when I was talking to her before. I'd hate her to wake up down there and find the children gone and not remember where they are. I think I'd better take a motel down there so that I can visit her each day with the children.'

'You made a deal with me less than an hour ago, Miss Haldane, and I expect you to fulfil that bargain. You said you would bring the children to the farm.' His voice was grim.

'I thought Michelle would be there with the children.' Shannon's brown eyes appealed to the doctor for support.

'Look, I know you've had a lot of travelling, but I suggest you go with James. You'll feel better after you've seen what a beautiful place it is—quiet and peaceful, modern and open. You're probably imagining those old dark brick horrors. Talk to the staff there and if they suggest it's better you stay, then do so. Be advised by them.'

'Yes, I'll do that.' She smiled at him. She knew he had understood her fears and was making it quite clear that there was no collusion between himself and James McCabe. She had been suspicious when he had asked James to take Michelle in the car. How convenient that he was all dressed, with the big station wagon ready to order.

'See you, James.' The doctor patted Shannon on the shoulder. 'You've been a good friend to that girl. I respect you for your loyalty and concern. Her recovery could depend on one person believing in her—having faith that she can make it. She needs someone to bat for her side. Ring me if you have any problems.'

He walked out, just as the enormity of her problem hit her. She had been counting on Michelle being at the farm. She had no idea how to care for two small children, not even the rudimentary knowledge of children's routine and diet.

She rushed out of the door and caught him at the car, and hastily explained her trouble. His broad smile was reassuring.

'Nothing to it, Miss Haldane. You'll do a fine job, but I'll give the local Health Nurse a ring tonight, and she can call at the farm in the morning and give you a few pointers. Now take that look off your face—she'll be very tactful. James won't know that it's a crash course. I wouldn't undermine your authority for worlds. James will think it's just a routine check-up, and will credit me with a truly professional attitude.'

Brad got into his car and gave her a wicked wink. 'I'll drop out myself from time to time . . . for purely professional reasons, you understand.' His admiring glance belied his words. 'Oh, and stop worrying about them not having a decent meal all day. They'll survive. Grab some fish and chips to eat on the way to Hokitika ... great nutritional value, and no washing up!'

Shannon watched him reverse smartly, and waved in response to his cheerful 'thumbs up' sign. She had a smile on her face as she went back to the motel. She felt comforted by his advice, and her ego was in fine shape, thanks to the implied compliment that she was worth visiting at the farm even if it was not for medical reasons.

Her smile was wiped off by James' sarcastic comment, 'So you couldn't resist trying to manipulate Brad to your way of thinking. He may be highly susceptible to a pretty girl, but I can assure you that he won't let your flirtatious manner sway his judgment.'

Shannon glared at him. The injustice of his remark really stung her, and she wanted to lash out violently at him, but caught the anxious look in Marigold's eyes, and controlled the urge ... with difficulty. There was no use upsetting the child, so she smiled sweetly and replied, 'Glad you think I'm pretty. It does a girl good to receive two compliments!'

She walked past him, not even trying to control her laughter at the anger revealed in his eyes. Serve him right!

'If you would pack Michelle's case we'd better get on the road immediately.' His tone was icy with contempt.

'There's nothing to pack. Michelle has brought nothing of her own with her.' Shannon picked up her own few things and packed them into her case and shut it before turning towards James, observing blandly, 'The children have only what they stand up in, and Joshua has only one change of nappies left.'

'I told you she was totally irresponsible.' The

words exploded from him. 'And you're no better. . . .'

Shannon went through to the room and collected Michelle's weekend bag without speaking. She knew she had been deliberately provocative. She put the wet nappies and dirty clothes in a separate plastic bag, then packed the unused groceries back into the carton. She caught Joshua and changed his nappies, and told Marigold to go through to the toilet, still ignoring James completely, but being fully aware of his furious scrutiny.

She was a little ashamed of her unhelpful attitude, but his own manners left room for enormous improvement. She hefted Joshua on her hip and took Marigold's hand before turning directly to face him, her gaze steady and unwavering. 'If you want my co-operation, you only have to ask for it. If you prefer to direct operations by yelling orders mingled with heavy sarcasm, I'll do my best to carry them out. You choose.'

His flint-blue eyes bored right through her, and she was never more conscious of her lack of inches. He towered over her, and her legs went rubbery as she felt the force of his barely controlled anger and frustration leap towards her with a violence that was more frightening than a physical attack. She held her stance, defying him with every ounce of her slender figure, chin up, and brown eyes flashing. She knew if she showed fear, he would treat her as dirt for the rest of her stay.

His voice came like a crack of a whip. '*You* demand courtesy, do you, Miss Haldane? Why, you interfering little. . . .'

She stepped towards him swiftly, her voice as hard and sharp as his had been. 'Not in front of the children, please, James. Remember their tender years.' Her lips curved into a wicked grin. 'My name is

Shannon. If we're to work closely together, it seems ridiculous to be so formal.'

She did not exactly run from the room, but she was moving fast.

Marigold protested, 'You're hurting my hand! You're holding it too tight.'

Shannon did not stop until she reached the station wagon, then she released Marigold's hand with a hasty apology, placed Joshua on the bonnet of the car and leaned weakly against it for support. What had possessed her to act in such an aggressive way? She hardly knew herself. That wretched McCabe man brought to the surface emotions she did not even know she owned, and that had been the second time today that she had felt like punching him on his oh, so handsome nose. *And* she had called him James in such a patronising manner. The enormity of her behaviour appalled her. Where had the ever so cool, well disciplined and co-ordinated Miss Haldane disappeared to? And where had this new and rather nasty personality been hiding all these years? Had it been there all the time, lurking beneath the surface, just waiting to be scratched?

She buried her face in Joshua's soft baby body and giggled weakly, and he responded with glee, chuckling as he grabbed handfuls of her hair with enough strength to bring tears to her eyes. Carefully she extricated herself, and tried to restore order to her hair and to her equilibrium. She had faced James McCabe like David challenging Goliath, and she was shocked to know that it had stimulated her, and excited her more than any other experience ever had.

She heard his firm purposeful footsteps approaching and immediately the adrenalin went coursing through her veins, keying every nerve in preparation for a battle.

'If you would open the back door, Shannon, I'll

put Michelle there. She should travel more comfortably lying down. I've borrowed a pillow and rug from the motel.' There was no emotion in his voice.

Shannon helped settle Michelle while he returned for the baggage.

She stood quietly with the children, waiting while he loaded the boot, and then offered politely, 'There's a car seat in my car for Joshua. I bought it this morning.' She handed him her keys.

He walked swiftly to her car, unclipped the seat and placed it in the middle of the front seat, then lifted Joshua into it, giving him an affectionate pat on the head. Then he picked Marigold up and seated her beside Joshua, and held the door open for Shannon. His face was stern, his eyes enigmatic, but he had complete control of himself now.

Warily Shannon slipped into her place, flicking a glance towards him, trying to gauge his mood. He had called her Shannon . . . was it to be a truce?

He stared down at her small erect figure for a moment, his eyes narrowed thoughtfully. 'I'd like to be around when you meet my father. It should be interesting. He's always maintained that it's not the size of the dog that counts, but the amount of fight that's in it.'

The door slammed, and Shannon watched his long lean powerful figure stride round the front of the station wagon. Had there been a touch of admiration in his voice? She leaned past Marigold to see him take his place behind the wheel, her brown eyes alert to detect any change in his expression. A hint of laughter could mean so much. You could survive any situation if there was a sense of humour shared. She found nothing . . . no softening. James ignored her and concentrated on reversing out of the parking lot.

She took Marigold on her knee and leaned back

against the very comfortable upholstery, trying to relax, but it was impossible. She was too aware of James McCabe. He was so arrogantly sure of himself, a genuine nine-carat-gold domineering male, and she could not control a crazy sense of exhilaration which flowed through her as she thought of the next few weeks in his company. She would make him back up, she would make him admit he was wrong to try and separate Michelle from her children. She was surprised and not a little intrigued by the intensity of her feelings. She had always been sane, reasoned, self-controlled, slightly objective and removed from all the high drama and emotion that had gripped her stepsisters throughout the past few years. She had always known her destiny was to roam the world, to be free, to run before the wind, so she had deliberately held herself aloof from attachments or involvements which could slow her down.

She had not believed that she had any deep and hidden emotional depths, but if something in James McCabe's personality had triggered off unknown qualities in her character, then he had better beware. James McCabe had better step aside while he was still in one piece!

CHAPTER FOUR

THEY had travelled only a short distance along a wide busy street when James swung into the kerb. He took out his wallet and handed Shannon several notes. 'There's sixty dollars there. Go into that chemist's shop and buy what you need in the way of toilet necessities for Michelle. Get the best. Take Marigold with you, I'll take Joshua. And make it fast. Then cross the street to that department store and we'll choose the rest of her requirements.'

Shannon stared at the money. 'It won't cost that much for soap and a toothbrush. . . .'

James was already on the street with Joshua in his arms. 'I said *everything* she needs—talc, perfume, any extras you think of, don't economise.' He checked on Michelle through the window and strode off down the street.

Shannon grabbed Marigold and hurried to the chemist's shop. As quickly as she could she chose a beautiful toilet bag, then added face-cloth and toothbrush, hairbrush, comb, mirror and manicure set. 'Marigold, do you know what kind of soap Mummy likes?' she asked.

'Yes.' Marigold pointed confidently to a well known line.

'Great! We'll take matching talcum and body splash. Now what about lipstick and make-up?'

Marigold circled the display counters quickly, pointing to perfume, then eyeliner, mascara, cleansing lotions, and waiting impatiently for Shannon to open the lipsticks and blushers so she could see the colours. As her confident finger touched each shade

Shannon added it to the collection. She had no notion of Michelle's preferences, but she was prepared to back Marigold's judgment.

'You're a gem, chicken. Let's pay for these and go and meet your uncle.'

They crossed the street arriving simultaneously with Joshua and James McCabe.

'I have an account here,' James informed her as she handed him the change. 'I'll go through and get a suitcase. You buy her several nighties, a bathrobe, and anything else you think she'll need.'

Shannon preceded him into the shop, feeling a little breathless. When he moved, he moved fast.

'Shannon!'

She turned at the peremptory call, and walked back to him with an enquiring upward glance.

'People will be quite curious about the advent of you and the children in my life. I would appreciate it if you wouldn't satisfy their curiosity.'

Shannon grinned. 'My lips are sealed. Your secret is safe with me.' She was annoyed with herself as she caught up on Marigold. She had been asked nicely. There had been no need for her to be smart-alecky . . . no need at all, but it had been irresistible. And he had been annoyed . . . she had seen that telltale cheek muscle flick.

'Now, Marigold, we have no time to dither. I'm going to let you help me choose Mummy's nighties, but only if you're fast. Does she like long ones or shorties? she added to Shannon.

'Shorties.'

'Good, that's one problem settled. Here they are on this rack. I'll flick them along and you say stop when you see one you think she'd like.'

Marigold stood back, her small head slightly on one side, and her eyes narrowed in concentration. 'Okay.' Three times she called 'Stop!' and her small face was wreathed in smiles as Shannon unhooked each exquisite froth of a gown and laid it over her arm. 'Oh! Mummy is going to be so excited!'

Shannon held back a sigh. Michelle was beyond excitement over clothes at the moment . . . but she would get well, and then she'd appreciate her daughter's fantastic taste. 'Now a robe. I'll carry these.'

'Put them straight into the case.' James opened it. 'Have you got everything?'

'Hardly. Come on, Marigold. Which one would Mummy choose?'

Impatiently James followed. 'Do you mean to say you're letting the kid choose?'

'She has excellent taste, and Michelle always lets her decide—she told me so yesterday. Watch her in action!' Shannon moved the elegant robes along the rack, dreams of lace and silk, quilted florals, tailored woollens.

'Stop!' Marigold walked forward and touched an attractive powder blue velvet flowing gown, trimmed with white fur.

'I think you'll have to choose again, love. That's the most expensive robe on the stand.'

'An excellent choice. Go over there and pick out a pair of matching slippers.' James dropped it into the case and followed the eager flitting figure.

Shannon trailed behind them and watched Marigold unerringly head for pale blue feathered mules, her small face flushed with joy as she held them up for James's approval. What a pity the day had to end with Michelle in hospital! She hoped the children did not take it too badly.

'Anything else?' James asked.

'Not that I can think of . . . oh handkerchiefs, I suppose. She'll be too tired to do any writing or craft work for a while. And I'll be close by if she needs anything else.'

'You'll be coming home with me to the farm, unless the hospital authorities state otherwise,' James told her harshly. 'Grab a dozen or so of the hankies and I'll get these written on my account.'

'I'd be better at a motel with the children,' Shannon protested. 'You won't have a cot or high-chair. . . .'

He turned back sharply. 'I've just ordered those very articles to be sent out home. They'll be there before we are. Have you bought nappies for this young man?'

Shannon flushed. 'Not yet. I haven't had time.' She was not willing to admit that she had completely forgotten them.

'What else do they need? I mean absolutely essential things. We'll bring them in tomorrow and outfit them with some gear.'

Shannon knew they had no nightclothes, but as they had slept in their underwear last night another night would not hurt. She instinctively knew that Marigold would take much longer choosing her own nightgown than she had her mother's, and she did not want to be too long away from Michelle.

'No, I'll manage until the morning . . . except for fish and chips, they're essential.'

'*Fish and chips!*' James shifted Joshua on to his other arm so that his disapproval could be more clearly visible to Shannon. 'You propose to feed these kids fish and chips?'

Shannon's brown eyes lit with laughter, and her crooked grin was impudent. 'Strictly on doctor's orders.' Why was there such joy in shocking him? She was behaving like a minx, but his anger brought an instantaneous response of laughter in her. Perhaps it was a defence mechanism!

He turned on his heel and strode to the counter.

'Afternoon, Jean. Would you put all these things on my account? The suitcase has already been entered.'

'Good afternoon, James. Lovely day, isn't it?' The woman picked up her receipt book and moved the carbon. 'You said your account?' She lifted out one of the flimsy nightgowns with a bright curiosity.

'Yes. And I'm in a hurry,' James replied in a voice which uncompromisingly stated he wasn't prepared to answer any questions. 'Wait for these, Shannon. I'll meet you at the car—and don't waste time with idle chatter.'

'Certainly, James,' she replied demurely, but as she met the warning in his flint-hard blue eyes, her own brimmed with amusement.

'Tell Jean to add a couple of packets of those disposable nappies to the order.' He marched out with Joshua, annoyance obvious in every movement of his athletic virile body.

She saw the woman named Jean turn and reach for the nappies and add them to the order. She realised that most people would automatically respond to James' air of authority. Maybe she was going to be the exception that proved the rule . . . the thought did not cause her a single qualm.

The assistant deftly clipped the price tags off and packed the clothes and completed the docket. 'Staying with James, are you?'

'Yes.' Shannon was non-encouraging, and felt a little badly about it. Jean looked such a friendly person.

'Been to the Coast before?' Jean asked as she clipped the suitcase shut.

'No, I haven't,' Shannon answered with a friendly smile, and took possession of the case. 'Come on, Marigold, we must hurry.

'Thank you—that's kind of you. Goodbye.' She walked out with pleasantly warmed feelings. Jean was naturally curious, and showed it, but there was also a kindness and genuine welcome in her voice.

At the car Shannon asked Michelle if she felt able to share the fish and chips.

'No, nothing. I just feel rotten. I just want to die.'

Again Shannon was swamped with an awful feeling of helplessness and fear. What if Michelle didn't get better? She tried to make her more comfortable on the seat. 'We'll soon be at the hospital, Michelle. You'll be better when you get your pills.' She knew she was saying it more to reassure herself than Michelle. 'Would you like Marigold to sit with you?'

Michelle shook her head.

Marigold pushed past Shannon to lean in by her mother. 'We've got you some lovely new clothes, Mummy. I picked them.'

'Go away. Just leave me alone. . . .' Michelle's voice was thin and tired.

Shannon closed the door with a sigh. 'Come on, pet, you sit in the front with me. Mummy's tired. She'll be so pleased about the things tomorrow. You wait and see!'

Marigold's face had lost its glow, and the fear was back in her big blue eyes. 'Are you real sure?'

Shannon seated herself in the front seat and took the little girl on her knee. 'Of course I'm sure! The doctor said to take Mummy to hospital just for a wee while and then she'll be all well, and come home to the farm. You'll love being at the farm, won't you? I'm sure Uncle James has lots of animals.'

'Will you be there, Shannon?'

'Yes, love, I'll be there, and Joshua . . . we'll have a lovely time.'

Tear-filled blue eyes fixed themselves on Shannon's face. 'And you won't leave us?'

Shannon kissed her and said fiercely, 'No, darling, I won't leave you till Mummy comes home again.'

The answer seemed to satisfy Marigold and she twisted around to watch up the street. 'Here comes James.'

'Uncle James,' Shannon corrected automatically. She must be crazy to make such a promise. But what else could she do? She couldn't leave these two children completely defenceless. Fear again clawed at her. . . . What if Michelle did not recover? Well, she was fully committed to them for the next six weeks anyway. She wouldn't back away from that. But after that. . . . Was it to be a lifetime commitment? Would she never be free to live her own life? She was disgusted at herself for these thoughts. She had promised Michelle; she had promised Marigold. How could she be so selfish as to be still hankering after her own concerns? If only James McCabe had been an ordinary loving man, prepared to take on Michelle and the children, she wouldn't be in this predicament. But there was nothing ordinary about James McCabe. He was rock-hard and determined to have his own way.

'Anyone hungry? Here, take these packets. I had them wrapped separately—no vinegar or salt on the children's. They smelt mouthwatering, so I got some for myself. Watch out, they're pretty hot.'

'Great!' Shannon reached out to accept the newspaper-wrapped meal, while James threaded Joshua back in his seat, and took his own place. What a flimsy character she was, one moment hating and resenting his arrogance, and the next moment being so grateful for the reassurance of his strength and competence. She might be irritated by his domineering ways, but oh, she was so glad to have someone to share the load with her. Was she beginning to have a sneaking admiration for the wretched McCabe? Heaven forbid! He was a monster, a cruel hard-hearted monster, completely without excuse.

He was trying to tear this small pathetic family apart and she, Shannon, was all that stood in his way. She had better keep the whole picture in its proper perspective, and not be sidetracked by a begrudgingly given feeling of appreciation, for a much-needed meal and a luxurious car ride.

As she blew on the delicious-tasting fish and chips to cool them for the impatient Joshua, she noted the smooth skilful way James handled the big station wagon. It was obvious he loved driving and had a flair for it. There, she was doing it again—admiring the strong tanned hands on the wheel. Oh, she would have to watch herself. But she had to admit he had style . . . something about the way he carried himself, the casual way he wore that oh, so expensive suit. Obliquely she studied his stern face, looking for some weakness. Carefully she fed Joshua another piece, and helped Marigold find a cooler chip, before returning to her study of James. She didn't like handsome men . . . they were too conceited. And he was handsome, she could not deny it. From the top of his head with its thick dark well-cut hair to the tip of his well-polished shoes he seemed to be without defect. It was disappointing. She wanted to find something to despise, something she could belittle, something which would make him less overpowering.

When she had taken the edge off the children's hunger, she opened one end of James' packet and offered it to him, then started on her own with wonderful enjoyment. She had not known how famished she was. It was delicious. By the time they had all finished and the papers were tucked away in the handy plastic rubbish container, she felt much more cheerful.

'Dr Brad Clark certainly knows the correct medicine to prescribe, doesn't he, Marigold? I think he's

a clever man, and he'll know how to make Mummy
all better too. If he knew we needed fish and chips
to make us happy, he'll know just what to give
Mummy.'

'Will you read me a story, Shannon?' Marigold
asked.

'Bother! I packed your books in the bag in the
boot.'

'Tell me one, then,' Marigold pleaded.

'Why don't you ask your Uncle James?' Shannon
suggested sneakily, shooting a taunting glance past
Joshua to watch James' reaction. 'If your Uncle
James feels he's capable of caring for two small children singlehanded, I'm sure he must have an endless
fund of good stories.'

'Would you, Uncle James? Please tell me a story!'

There was a long silence, then James cleared his
throat. 'Okay. I'll tell you a true story about your
father when he was a little boy, not much bigger
than you are now.'

Shannon sat seething as she listened to his firm
deep voice relating an exciting and interesting ad-
venture about Mark following a little used track
away into the bush, and how he had played by a
stream and all the animals he met, and how he had
become tired and fallen asleep, while everyone had
gone frantic at the farm searching for him. The story
ended happily with an old farm dog who loved Mark
tracking him down and bringing him home safely.
Marigold sat enthralled, her eager eyes glued to the
big man's face.

That was why Shannon was furious. She had
meant to put James in a difficult spot, and he had
come through it with flying colours. Didn't he ever
feel inadequate?

Marigold gave a satisfied sigh. 'That was perfect!'
And it had been too, Shannon thought grumpily

as she lifted the grizzling Joshua from his seat and transferred Marigold into it. She found Joshua's bottle, popped it in his mouth and cradled him lovingly. James McCabe was no slouch. He had told that story well, intelligently gearing it to Marigold's age without scaring her about being lost in the bush but emphasising the delights of a country upbringing, and underlining that he had shared her father's childhood. Shannon felt the story had been as much for her as it had been for Marigold.

She glanced across and saw him smile at Marigold, and was amazed at the transformation it made to the granite-like features of his face. Why, he almost appeared human! His hard blue gaze held hers for a second, challenging her, then with a flicker of contempt he returned his eyes to the road. She shivered. He knew exactly why she had thrust the story request on to him, and he knew that he had coped supremely well and had won Marigold's confidence as well.

He was despicable. He was beneath contempt. He would use any method within his power to win these children. And what would happen to them if he gained his objective and secured their love and affection? He would use it to prove that they had no need of their mother. He was ruthlessly sure of his ability to bring them up and was contemptuous of anything Shannon might do to interfere with his plans. He had everything on his side—wealth, power, position, and now possession, because she had foolishly allowed him to manipulate her into taking the children to the farm. Even the law was on his side ... they had already agreed to his having the custody of them, even if it wasn't accomplished formally yet.

Shannon bit her lip. Where was her courage now? She must have been mad to think that she could

turn him aside from his purpose. She had boasted to
Michelle that she could make him step aside, she
had boasted to herself that she could make him back
up, but if she was completely honest, the more she
got to know him the more remote seemed the chance
that she could sway his decision by any attitude or
appeal or argument.

'We're almost there,' James said. 'Have you told
Marigold the programme?'

Startled, Shannon looked about her. Had she
travelled an hour and a half without noticing?
'Where are we? Yes, Marigold knows her mother is
going to stay in hospital for a few days.' She gave
Marigold a warm reassuring smile before turning to
check on Michelle. 'We're in Hokitika,' she told her.
'The hospital is away up on the hill above the town.'

'You *said* you'd *stay* with us,' Marigold demanded
anxiously.

'For sure I will, pet. We'll just take Mummy in
and put her in a lovely bed, wearing her pretty
nightie, and with really kind nurses to look after her.
Which nightie do you think she should wear first?'

'The green one,' Marigold replied quickly.

'Right, the green one.' It was easy to divert
Marigold's thoughts, but her own were a different
matter. She suddenly felt choked up with worry over
leaving Michelle behind. Would they be kind to her?
Would they understand her fears? Could they give
her back her will to live?

It was only as James changed gears and the car
started up the steep hill that she became aware of
her surroundings, and the glory of the setting sun on
the sweeping coastline, the shining waves of the
Tasman Sea pounding on the beach, the bush-clad
hills, and the sky suffused with colour, and the maj-
estic Alps rearing high, their harsh jagged peaks
biting into the soft apricot glow.

He swung round and parked near a palm tree in a wide gravel drive. Shannon braced herself, not wanting to arrive. As he got out she stared out at the immaculate lawns and gardens, and the attractive buildings, but nothing reassured her. She felt fear grip her like a physical force. She was so ignorant of any form of psychiatric medicine. What were their methods? What were their success rates? Oh, she knew people had breakdowns and recovered, but this wasn't just people . . . this was Michelle.

Her door opened and James stood with the new case in his hand. 'You all right?'

'Yes,' she answered, angry at the wobble so evident in her voice.

'Do you want to go in with Michelle or would you rather stay here with the kids?'

More than anything in the world she wanted to stay with the children, but that would be like running out on a friend. 'I'll go in with her. Do you think she can walk?'

'Yes, I can.' Michelle spoke from the back seat in a surprisingly determined voice. 'Just give me a minute.'

James took hold of Joshua and as Shannon got out of the car he caught her arm. 'She'll be all right here, you have my word.' He spoke low so that Michelle could not hear. He picked up the case. 'Take as long as you want. The kids and I will go walk-about. It will be good for them to be out of the car for a bit.'

While Shannon helped Michelle from the car, James walked across to a ramp and put the case down, then walked back towards them. He waited without awkwardness as Michelle kissed both children, then he picked one up in each arm as if they were featherweights, and walked away promising them a special treat: he mentioned goldfish.

Shannon was more grateful than she cared to admit that he had handled the parting so well, and she walked slowly towards the admittance door with Michelle leaning against her. She held clutched in her hand the admittance note that James had given her. He also explained that Brad had said they were to go directly to the ward as the administration staff had left for the day.

As they entered the corridor a Sister in uniform came forward. 'Welcome. You'll be Mrs McCabe from Reefton. We've been expecting you.' Suddenly she stopped speaking and stared intently at Michelle. 'Why, I know you! You're Michelle. You poor wee scrap, what's the world being doing to you?' She wrapped her arms about the slender girl and hugged her.

'Oh, Sister Jones, it's so lovely to see you!' Michelle smiled through her tears.

'No tears now, love. We'll have you right in no time.' Sister Jones turned to Shannon. 'Just wait in my office, while I get Michelle into bed, then I'll come back and talk with you.'

Shannon walked into the office and was glad to sit down, her legs were so shaky, but she felt miles better. That Sister Jones had such a warm compassionate manner, and it was obvious she liked Michelle. It was such a relief to think she was leaving her amongst friends . . . caring friends. Why, she had forgotten that Michelle had told her she originally came from Hokitika. This Sister wouldn't be the only one who knew her. From farther down the corridor she heard the sound of laughter and teasing, and relaxed even more. If this place had a happy atmosphere she wouldn't mind so much leaving Michelle. Why she had developed such a strong protective feeling for Michelle really puzzled her. That also was out of character. Yes, she had loved the girls, and had felt responsible for them, but this was different. If she thought anyone would coerce or bully her . . . well, she'd come in swinging. Maybe it was because Michelle was so forlorn and fragile, or maybe it was because she had saved her once and didn't want anything or anyone pressuring Michelle to the point of no return again.

Sister Jones bustled in and seated herself comfortably at her desk. 'Thank you for being so patient. I wanted to stay with Michelle until she was settled.'

'Can I see her to say goodbye, please?' Shannon asked anxiously.

'No, I don't think that would be advisable. She'll be asleep by now, and she needs that more than anything. We've given her something to help—do you understand?'

'Yes.' Shannon knew her eyes were filling with tears and she tried to hold them back, but failed. It had been a long, hard and very exhausting day, and she had so much wanted to state to Michelle once again that the children were safe with her. She had thought if she said it just as she left, that it might stick in Michelle's mind.

'Are you a relation of Michelle's? Did I get your name?' Sister Jones leaned forward sympathetically. 'I wish you wouldn't upset yourself. She's in our hands now. We'll take good care of her. When you see her in a few days' time you'll be amazed at her progress.'

Shannon fumbled for a handkerchief and blurted out, 'A few days? Can't I see her tomorrow? I'll get a motel down here, and then she can see the children every day. She needs the children.'

'That's exactly what she doesn't need. She needs rest and quiet and no worries. Trust me, I know what I'm talking about.' The Sister's voice was firm and final. She pulled a form forward. 'Dr Clark gave me most of the details, but not your name.'

'I'm not a relation, I'm just a friend. My name is
Shannon Haldane. I haven't known Michelle long.
Look, I'm sorry to make a fuss, but she did try to
kill herself . . . only yesterday. It was because her
children were being taken away. She gave me the
children to care for. What if she wakes up and
doesn't remember where they are? It could make
her try again.'

'It could, but now I know what the problem is I'll
be able to reassure her. Give me your address and
phone number, and if she wants to, Michelle may
ring you and speak to the children—that's a
promise.'

Hesitatingly Shannon gave James' name and
address, but could not remember the number.

'That's fine—we'll look it up in the book. How
many children has she?'

'Two. Marigold is four, and Joshua is just one.'

'Lovely names! When you come visiting I want to
meet them. I've known Michelle since she was a little
girl, and I was a great friend of her grandmother's.
I'm so pleased to see she has a good friend. You've
taken on a big task, but I'm sure you're very capable.
Will you not trust us to do our task just as consci-
entiously?'

Something of the Sister's calmness flowed over
Shannon, and she stopped crying. 'Forgive me for
being so stupid. I know she's beyond my help.'

'That's good. Now may I offer you a cup of tea?
Or would you like to look through the complex?
Perhaps if you saw and spoke to some of the patients
you wouldn't feel so badly.'

Shannon stood up. 'No, thank you. You've been
most kind. Now, I must get back to the children.'

The Sister walked to the door with her, giving a
friendly pat on the shoulder as she said goodbye.

'Michelle will be fine. You may ring each day if you wish, and we'll let you know the moment she's allowed visitors.'

Shannon walked towards the car with a lighter step. It seemed to make such a difference that she could ring each day. She was surprised to see it was almost dark. James was in the car with the children.

She opened the door, and the inside light showed her her face pale and strained, her brown eyes enormous with recent tears. 'Sorry I was away so long.'

'That's all right. It couldn't have been easy. The kids have been very good, but they're tired now. Shut the door and we'll be on our way. It'll be good to get home.'

Shannon closed the door without answering. She was completely drained. She noticed the car seat was gone, and looked enquiringly at James.

'Joshua wore himself out staggering around the goldfish pond trying to catch the fish and I knew it wouldn't be long before he fell asleep, and I was right. I'll slide him on to the seat between us, he'll be more comfortable there. Marigold wanted to cuddle down where her mother had been, so I let her. You'll have a more restful trip home.'

With mixed feelings Shannon watched him put the baby down and cover him with a jersey, then he switched on the stereo and drove slowly down the hill and out on to the main road.

He had said 'Let's go home' as if it meant home was a dear and comfortable place. Well, it might mean that to him, but Shannon would bet it wouldn't be too comfortable for her. It was unknown territory, and James would be master. He had the makings of a real lord of the manor. Home to her was the house in Wellington, and William and the girls. Home was a gracious residence with well tended grounds and a gardener, and Mrs McPhail who helped out three mornings a week, while Shannon had played receptionist to William's patients. Oh dear, she should have thought of Simon first, before Mrs McPhail . . . no, she should not. Simon would be no use with the children and she'd trade him off any day to have help three mornings a week.

Was she getting homesick already? *That was ridiculous.* Only one day away and she was yearning to get back to the familiar. What about her craze for freedom, her dream to run before the wind? Was she really a stay-putter, not a go-getter? Could she have been that wrong about herself?

She felt the powerful car pick up speed, and closed her eyes, letting the music soothe her. Sleep seemed irresistible in the warmth and luxury of the car, but she struggled against it. She didn't want to relax in the company of James; he was too dangerous an adversary. She wished he had not taken down the car seat; she wanted to erect barriers between them, not dismantle them. She had seen the children succumb to his charm in just a few hours . . . she didn't want to join them. It was so easy to feel gratitude for the way he had coped with the children, even settling them to sleep so that she could have a restful trip. It was easy to be grateful for his sensitivity in letting her go into the hospital with Michelle. It was easy to be grateful for the generous way he had provided everything for Michelle, spending freely, giving only the best. Most of all it was so easy to feel grateful for the sheer physical strength of the man, the way he had carried Michelle to the car from the motel, the way he had hardly felt the weight of Joshua.

How could she have coped without him? The thought daunted her. The day would have ended in disaster without him. He was rock-hard, yet they had all been protected and secure behind that rock.

It would be fatally easy to abdicate, and let him make all the decisions. Fatal because his motives were suspect—more than that, evil. It was wicked to think of separating Michelle from her children. As long as she kept James' purpose in the forefront of her mind, she could resist him ... and she would, till her last breath.

She was drifting to sleep, but she fought it. ... Her eyelids closed.

CHAPTER FIVE

SHANNON glanced at the calendar as she cleared the dinner dishes off the table, and was astonished to realise that two of her six weeks had already gone. It was absolutely incredible. Where had they gone? And she had meant to write to the family, but she never had a spare minute. She would write tonight. She would have so much to tell them, about Michelle, about the children, about James McCabe . . . mostly about James McCabe.

No, she wouldn't tell them much about James, because she really didn't know much about him. How could she actually live in a house for two whole weeks with him and know so little of him? Her brown eyes shone with amusement as she plunged her hands into the warm soapy water, beginning to wash the dishes. She knew the reason why she knew so little. Because he worked at it, not letting her know, and he was good at it. He learned a great deal about her, about William and the girls, even about Simon, whom he referred to as her tame lawyer, but she learned nothing in return.

Her grin widened, as she began to dry the plates and stack them away. His steel blue eyes never missed a trick, but he gave nothing away . . . nothing about his private life. He intrigued her, because he wasn't the strong silent type at all. He told the children endless stories about himself and Mark and their sister Louise, when they were children. He talked to her about the farm and about the district, about the whole province if it came to that. But about himself he was like a clam. Shannon was smiling because she could not help admiring how deft and skilful he was at avoiding anything personal, but now and again when she really needled him with her laughter, his blue eyes would flash with fire and he would show the resentment he felt towards her, for interfering with his well laid schemes. And she would have been lying if she said she didn't enjoy taking the mickey out of him.

It was irresistible, the desire to dent that suave, sophisticated image he presented. Shannon hung up the tea-towel, wiped down the stainless steel sink bench, and checked the large comfortable kitchen to see that all was tidy before joining James and the children in the lounge. She liked this kitchen. It had all the labour-saving devices she needed, but it wasn't madly modern. She liked the house too, large and roomy, with a wide verandah and plenty of space for the children to play. And they had settled in so well, it was truly amazing. Amazing, too, that she had settled in just as happily.

She just loved the house from the moment she arrived. It was a large rambling farmhouse in need of a coat of paint. The furniture was old and shabby, but very comfortable. The curtains and covers were clean but faded, yet the atmosphere was pleasant and welcoming. The carpets were good, the furniture solid and well chosen. Once it had been a very happy home, well loved, but there were strange gaps, no ornaments or photographs around, and squares on the wall showing where pictures had once hung. The lawns were well kept but the large garden neglected and forlorn. It had a waiting air about it, and it delighted Shannon to put a few feminine touches to it, giving it a more lived-in feel. She felt much of its character came from two beautiful stained-glass windows at the end of the lounge and two elegant palm trees on the front lawn.

It wasn't isolated as she had feared, but quite near the main road, and people waved as they drove by—but none of them stopped. Obviously James was a recluse. She saw neighbouring houses only a mile or so away, and there was a house quite near on a plateau behind the house, but she never saw people there. She wasn't lonely; the children kept her too busy for that.

If she was truly honest with herself she would say she had never been more content in her life—well, except for the tension between her and James, and the ever-present concern over Michelle. They had been down three times to visit Michelle, and while she wasn't worse, she wasn't a great deal better. He never went in to see her and James could have been much more difficult if he'd put his mind to it. He was courteous, helpful, generous and usually perfectly controlled.

'I could have given you a hand with the dishes, Shannon.' James spoke from the armchair near the open fire.

Marigold was curled up on his knee, which was *her* place while he watched the six-thirty news on T.V. each evening. 'I could help too.'

'You help me a lot, Marigold, I think it's good for you to have a rest after your bath and tea. And you too, James. You put in such a long day on the farm, it's only right that you should have your share of the children after dinner.' Shannon turned several small jerseys which she had airing on the wire guard in front of the glowing pot-bellied stove. 'I love this stove.'

Joshua came crawling rapidly towards her with a busy-bee whirring along behind him. 'Don't you think he's terrific, learning to do that? I've never seen a baby do that before. He only learned it today.' Shannon picked him up and hugged him, but he

struggled to get down. As soon as she put
him on the floor he caught the bead on the end of
the string in his mouth and off he went towards the
far end of the room, showing off his skill for
James.

'He's the greatest,' James agreed, leaning down to
pat the sparkling-eyed baby.

Shannon went to the old colonial couch and sat
down, waiting for the nightly ritual. The children
seemed to have worked out a sharing agreement on
James. Marigold had him until the news was
finished, then he would switch off the T.V. and play
the piano for them—well, for Joshua really, then
finish off with a romp on the floor with both of
them.

As she picked up her knitting, Joshua suddenly
tired of his toy and abandoned it, then, pulling himself up beside a small occasional table near James,
he climbed on to it, knelt up and clapped his hands.
He did it with such a comical air of confidence that
they would all be enthralled that it set them all
laughing.

'Must be time to switch off the T.V.' James got
up and carefully deposited Marigold in the big chair
and straightened her nightgown. 'You're beautiful
tonight, Marigold. You smell good too.' He ruffled
her light brown hair affectionately.

'That's Shannon's talc. She lended me some. She
smells good too.'

'I'll take your word for that.' James picked up
Joshua and came to put some wood on the stove,
carefully avoiding looking at Shannon. He must have
known she would be smiling.

'I had this stove put in a couple of years ago when
the power prices soared sky-high,' he told her. 'It's a
real boon. We rarely shut the sliding door between
the kitchen and lounge, and they're both big rooms,

so it's ideally placed here at the corner of the right angles.'

'It sends out a terrific heat, and there's oodles of hot water. It must save you a lot of money.'

'It does.' He stopped in front of her. 'Here, hold Joshua while I get this jersey off. It's mighty hot in here, but Marigold pleaded for an open fire. She wanted to watch the fir-cones you collected today go up in smoke.'

'We had great fun getting those. That wheelbarrow has a wonky tyre and I nearly ran over your best dog, two wekas, and your station agent who came round the corner in his car unexpectedly. He turned quite pale!' Shannon giggled as she remembered.

'He told me,' James said angrily. 'He thought he'd nearly killed you all. Life's just one hell of a joke to you, isn't it? Don't you ever take anything seriously?'

'Rubbish—they were perfectly safe.' She was stung by his sudden change of mood. They rarely snarled at each other in front of the children, and the criticism was unwarranted.

She stood up and shoved Joshua back into his arms, her eyes fierce. 'Yes, there are some things I do take seriously. For instance, the way you're butter-soft with the children, and so granite-hard with their mother. And . . . and every time you go near town you come home with another toy for each one. What are you trying to do . . . buy their love?'

She ran through to her room, gulping back her tears. Miserable McCabe, he'd made her do it again! She had been hitting below the belt with that remark about the toys, and she'd been as unfair as he had been. She found her hanky and wiped away her tears. She was stupid to be upset, but she prided herself on being fair, and she knew you couldn't buy Joshua's love. It just flowed out of him to everyone. Well, she wouldn't apologise; he never did when he hurt her.

She went in and turned back the beds ready for the children. James did everything so well. This cot, for example. It had been standing in the kitchen that first night they got home, completely made up, lambskin rug, pillow, sheets, blankets, and a huge Teddy bear, and a doll for Marigold. Shannon wouldn't have even known how to make up a baby's bed, but she needn't have worried. James commanded in town, it was waiting when he got home. All they had to do was drop Joshua in it, and carry it through to the room. Joshua hadn't even woken up. She sniffed inelegantly. She had never been *drawn* to people who were over-efficient.

She went back into the lounge and picked up her knitting. Marigold ran to climb on her knee for a cuddle, her small face anxious. 'I love you, Shannon.'

Shannon kissed her. 'I love you too, Marigold. You've no idea how much.'

'Do you love James too?'

'Not as much as you do,' Shannon answered very, very carefully.

James threw back his head and roared with laughter, and she fought not to join in, and lost.

It was the first time she had ever heard him laugh, and he had a nice laugh.

He spun round on the piano stool and faced her, still smiling. 'That was an excellent dinner you cooked tonight. I really do appreciate your efforts. It certainly is a wonderful change from bachelor life!'

He completed the turn, and continued to play, his strong tanned hands so sensitive and skilful on the keys. Joshua sat absolutely still on the thick sheepskin rug, gazing up in silent adoration as he always did. It was the only time he was ever still or quiet. Music seemed to hold a special magic for him.

James ended with a lovely Rod Stewart tune. It was a few years old, but some of the words held that haunting appeal. 'You'll be my breath when I grow old.'

Had he once loved someone like that? Something told Shannon that it had a special significance for him. It was a more tender touch on the keys, a softness, a gentleness. What had she been like? What would it be like to be loved like that by James? Wonderful—it would be wonderful. Unexpectedly she caught sight of her expression in the mirror above the piano, and turned sharply away. Horrified, she knew that it was a replica of the one on Joshua's small face—a look of awe and undisguised love. Ah, this couldn't happen to her, no, it couldn't. She never wanted to fall in love with anyone. And of all the men in the whole world she *didn't* want to fall in love with most, she would nominate James McCabe.

It couldn't happen like this, it couldn't happen to her. She had watched the girls fall in and out of love with incredible consistency but they had been willing and eager for love, watching for it, waiting for it, anxious for it to come their way. What had caused it? His laughter . . . so unexpected? His head thrown back, laughing with her? Was that all it needed? That was crazy. Or was it the compliment about the meal? He had thanked her before, he was always polite, but this time it was different, because he had laughed with her, almost as if they were friends. No, it was different because it had been offered almost as an apology for yelling at her.

Gosh, she really was a pushover! James only had to laugh with her, and *almost* apologise, and she fell instantly, six fathoms deep in love with him. She was shocked. She was furious. It was an insult to her intelligence to let such a thing happen. Her cheeks were burning. Well, he'd blame that on the stove. How could she be so *pathetic*!

'You're holding me too tight,' Marigold protested.

'Sorry.' Shannon released her so that she could go and join the other two in a rough-and-tumble on the carpet.

She wanted to shout and scream with rage. She knew she was even looking at James with different eyes. His strong, well-muscled body was lean and taut, and she was wondering what it would be like to be held in those arms, to be kissed by those lips, to be caressed by those hands. Her whole body throbbed with a new energy that came from deep within her, a longing and a desire that was new and frightening, yet exciting.

She stood up and walked swiftly into the kitchen, feeling restless, unable to sit still, wanting to walk, wanting to run, wanting to sing, wanting to dance. She bit her soft underlip and wrapped her arms about her slender figure, trying to control her trembling awareness that a new and vibrant force was exploding within her.

'Time these youngsters were in bed,' James called.

Time, that was what she needed. Time before she faced him, time to sort herself out. She felt betrayed by her body. . . . Think, think, *think*. It would go, it would disappear. She had watched Cushla be struck all of a heap several times, walking round dewy-eyed and half hypnotised, and she had recovered . . . well, until the last fatal dose which had never worn off, so she had taken a husband. It was just chemistry, a purely physical attraction. She did not deny the strength of it, this wild pulsating liquid fire that ran through her veins, but it wasn't a lethal dose. It could be controlled, restricted, tamed, and put to death.

'Coming,' she answered, feeling proud of her voice sounding so natural. She caught Joshua up and managed to hold his squirming body still long enough to change his nappies and pull on his diminutive pyjama pants.

'Phew! He's a tiger to hold down.'

She avoided looking at James, knowing her face was flushed with colour, but anyone who had struggled with Joshua would look the same. She knew he was standing right behind her with Marigold in his arms, waiting to follow her into the children's room. Each night he stayed with her to hear their prayers, to kiss them goodnight. As he sat on Marigold's bed gently stroking her cheek, Shannon felt a surge of envy swamp her, and shuddered at where her thoughts were leading. She pecked each child quickly on the cheek and left him to it, almost running from the room.

James came back to the kitchen and glanced at her.

'Good, you've got the kettle boiling, I'll get the cups. Joshua didn't settle too well, he seems a bit flushed. So do you—this room is far too hot. I'll open the passage door and let the heat get away.'

If only it were that simple! Shannon thought desperately. 'I'll make the coffee, and bring it through in a minute.' She didn't want him standing around near her. And this was always the danger period in their day, when the children went to bed, and there was no barrier between them. Usually she enjoyed it, sharing a relaxed cup of coffee, stimulated by the knowledge that she could fire a few barbed remarks at him, without upsetting the children. But not tonight.

'I'm tired,' she announced as she handed him his coffee. 'I'll go to bed as soon as I finish this.' What would she do with all those endless hours of darkness? Sleep had never been farther from her mind.

'Are the children too much for you? You're only a little slip of a thing. I could get help. . . .'

'I don't want any help. I'm as strong as a horse.' Shannon knew she sounded belligerent.

James shrugged his shoulders and turned to read the newspaper, then turned back, 'They're fantastic kids, aren't they? Are all children like that?'

How his face softened when they talked of the children! 'No. I think we're lucky. I think they're very special children.'

'I do too.' He started to read again.

Shannon sat watching his strong profile, the hard clean line of his jaw, the way his thick dark hair fell across his forehead as he bent forward, and his mouth, his lips . . . what would it feel like . . .?

She jumped to her feet. 'I'm off to bed.'

James looked up in surprise. 'That sounded like a declaration of war! Go, by all means, I won't interfere. Oh, by the way, I'll not be here for lunch tomorrow. A relative of mine wants me to look at a farm for him. I'll get away about eleven.'

'Do you have relatives around here?' She couldn't restrain her curiosity.

'A few,' he answered cryptically.

'They've never visited. Wouldn't they like to see Mark's children?'

'I warned them not to visit.' He looked at her carefully for a moment. 'I would like the children to go to church with us on Sunday. Think you could manage that? It's a ten o'clock service. The Bishop will be there, and I have to read the lesson.'

'A man of many parts,' she offered sarcastically. 'Are we going to the hospital in the afternoon?'

'Yes.'

'Is the farm near here? The one you're going to

look at?' She was angry with herself for prolonging this conversation. She must be schizophrenic—half of her wanted to rush to her room and bury herself under the blankets and the other half couldn't resist being near him.

'Up north—not far.'

'You're a mine of information,' she taunted.

He folded the paper meticulously before answering sardonically. 'I thought you were going to bed. I must apologise. I didn't know you were yearning for a little chat. I'm flattered. What will we discuss? The weather? Winter is very near . . . probably next week. There's fresh snow on the Alps.'

Her eyes glinted. 'Do you have a long winter?'

'You won't see the end of it. You'll be long gone,' he said abruptly.

'So will the children, because when I go so do they,' Shannon flung at him angrily.

In one lithe movement he was out of his chair and towering over her.

'Someone's knocked at the door!' she almost yelled, panicking a little at his fierce reaction.

James glared at her, then walked swiftly to the front door and opened it. 'Oh, it's you, Brad. Come on in. It'll be good to have a bit of intelligent conversation.'

Brad came in, smiling as usual. 'Hi, Shannon. Was that aimed at you? How cruel! Did I interrupt something important?'

'Nothing that won't keep,' James told him grimly. 'Take a seat. Shannon, get Brad some coffee.'

'Hi, Brad, nice to see you.' Shannon went to get the coffee. Brad had been out a couple of evenings after surgery, and she really enjoyed his company. And she could talk to him about Michelle. He didn't mind sharing her worries, and always made her feel more cheerful about Michelle's recovery.

She brought in three fresh mugs of coffee. With Brad here she felt safe from herself.

'Thanks, Shannon. How are the children?'

'Fine . . . oh, Joshua's a bit flushed and restless. It's not like him. I've just been in to cover him again.'

'I'll look at him before I go—probably teething. Then you two will be in for a bit of fun, walking the floor at nights and all that. Some children cut teeth the hard way, colds, bad ears, runny noses, off their tucker, grizzly. . . .'

'Cheer us up a bit more,' James interrupted.

'You didn't let me finish,' Brad protested. 'Some do it easy, just one bad night. I'll put some dope on the bus in the morning, you'd better have it handy.'

'Feel like a game of chess?' James suggested, after he had learned all he could about teething problems.

'Yes, wouldn't mind at all. I'm getting a bit rusty. How about you, Shannon? Do you know the game?'

'I'm brilliant,' Shannon said with a grin. 'I'll take you on after you've played James.'

James gave her a curious glance. 'I didn't know you played chess.'

'You never asked me. There's lots about me you don't know. I have many hidden talents. You just think you know everything.'

'That will do,' Brad said peaceably. 'You can play the winner, Shannon, and I know who it'll be. James plays a cracking game—beware.'

He would, Shannon thought resentfully, but she just might surprise him. Her stepfather loved chess, it had been his only hobby, and he had taught and coached her. She didn't just play social chess. Her eyes shone at the thought of a good challenge.

They set up the board, but before play started Brad remarked, 'James isn't the only one who doesn't know all about you. The whole town is a-hum with curiosity, you're a real mystery woman to them. I haven't let on that I know you at all, they'd soon wheedle it out of me. I'm putty in their hands. It's not idle curiosity, they're a friendly bunch.'

'I know,' Shannon said ruefully. 'When I drive in to get milk and groceries, they come at me from every angle—am I staying long, am I a relative, where do I come from? But James threatened me with violence if I became chatty on these trips, so I'm nearly as deft as he is at avoiding personal details. It's a shame too, because I'd love to be open and friendly. I think James is ashamed of us.'

'I don't think it's that,' Brad argued. 'You're a cute-looking trio, running about in that Yellow Peril. Marigold is such a sweetie, Joshua a right manly figure and if I may say so as a serious student of anatomy, you're stacked in a delightful package. The guy who invented jeans must have had your shape in mind.'

'Get away,' Shannon replied easily. 'You'll break the shovel handle.'

Brad laughed. 'I'm not laying it on too heavy— every word is true. Of course, you know that if they don't get told what they're itching to know, they'll make up a much more interesting version. I heard one the other day which I thought was quite original.'

'You shouldn't listen to gossip.' James said sharply.

'Tell me,' Shannon pleaded, leaning towards him, laughing.

'Right. Well, they know the kids are McCabes, so they think you're James' de facto wife. That he's been keeping you in style over the hill, and nipping over to have a bit on the side whenever he's lonely.

It's really an out for all those frustrated females who have tried to catch him.'

Shannon was outraged. 'They think I've . . . they think! How dare they! I'm going to tell them I've never met him before. Don't they think I've got any taste or discernment? I wouldn't have James McCabe served up on toast. I'm *fussy*!'

And again James threw back his head and roared laughing, and the sound melted her very bones. Brad joined him, the tears running down his face.

'It's not all that funny,' Shannon protested angrily. 'It's all right for you, James, makes you look a bit of a gay blade, but what about my reputation! You pair of idiots!'

She grabbed the coffee mugs and headed for the kitchen. Were these weird goosebumps going to break out every time he laughed? This tingling trembling torrent of sensuousness, which flooded her very being, left her weak and humiliated. You couldn't fall in love with someone you didn't like or trust. Not with a man whose heart was a lump of rock, a *child stealer*. She didn't admire dominating men. Brad and Simon were the sort of men who appealed to her, perceptive, straightforward and good humoured. James was selfish, vain and enigmatic. Oh, maybe he did have one or two good points, but they were hardly worth mentioning.

She went back and sat beside Brad and watched the game, and was relieved to note it was fairly amateur. She'd polish off Mighty McCabe with no trouble. Serve him right! He'd see who was the weaker sex. After her assessment she had trouble following the game to its conclusion. Her mind kept whirling with the most unusual thoughts. It was easy to see what had happened. She had watched James so closely, trying to get inside his mind, trying to discover what his plans for Michelle and the children were, so that she could frustrate them, and now she was suffering from a whiplash injury. She had followed too close, and crashed into an immovable object, and their position was reversed—he had got inside her head.

The trouble was, he was so big, physically and mentally. His personality was overpowering; she was aware of him every minute of the day, whether he was in the house or out on the farm. The whole household revolved around him—mealtimes, bedtimes, bathtimes. Joshua howled in anguish whenever James left for work, and both children went into raptures whenever he returned. All the telephone calls were for him, all the visitors, all the mail. There was no way that she would be able to put him out of her mind.

'Check and mate,' James said decisively.

'I've been trounced, Shannon,' groaned Brad. 'Can you get revenge for me? I'd better be on my way, I've been expecting a call all evening—must have been what put me off my game. Let's have a look at Joshua before I go.'

They walked to the bedroom together, and Joshua was uncovered and down the wrong end of the cot. Brad moved him back gently, 'Hmm, he's a bit feverish. See that red patch on his cheek, that's teething for sure. Hope you're not in for a bad night. I'll send that stuff out on the first bus.'

'I'm glad you told me it's only teething,' said Shannon. 'I would have been frantic if he'd got sick in the middle of the night and I didn't know why.'

They stepped back into the kitchen. 'Call me any time, Shannon. You're very quiet tonight. James getting you down? You need an antidote to all that virility, could be dangerous in a confined space. How about a date?'

'I'd rather have an inoculation.' Shannon spoke without thinking.

'Whew! Like that, is it? *Dynamite!* I hope it's not incurable, for your sake. He's a dedicated bachelor.' Brad's tone was sympathetic.

'It's curable. I didn't mean . . . you won't say anything. Promise?' Her pleading brown eyes were frantic.

Brad winked at her. 'Forget it. But I do think you need to get out occasionally. How about a game of golf tomorrow? Look, you couldn't help it, it was inevitable. Put two healthy specimens of the human race together so much and, psychologically speaking. . . .'

'You leave psychology out of it,' Shannon said, blushing furiously.

'What's up out there?' James called from the lounge. 'Is Joshua all right?'

'He's fine,' Brad assured him, walking through with Shannon trailing him nervously. 'I was just trying to get Shannon to come and have a game of golf tomorrow. Will you let her off the leash? She needs to get out of the house for a bit.'

'I won't,' James replied calmly. 'I'll be away tomorrow afternoon, she'll have to be with the children.'

'But I could get someone in town to watch them,' Brad protested. 'She must get some time off. Being cooped up. . . .'

'Has she been complaining?' James interrupted sharply.

'No. She's not, I am. What about Sunday?'

'No dice,' James told him. 'Church in the morning, Hokitika in the afternoon. Sit down, Shannon, I've set up the pieces.'

Shannon sat down and studied the board. She was going to win this game, and she needed to.

Brad stood watching the first few moves, then touched Shannon's cheek lightly. 'Cheerio. Looks like James has cornered the market on your time, which isn't fair, because he's not a prospective buyer and I am. I'll be back again. See you, James.'

Shannon waved to him, then turned back to concentrate on the next move. She was beginning to be very suspicious. After the first dozen moves she knew she had a tiger by the tail. James was no amateur. He was playing as well as William ever had, and maybe a little better. He had been very crafty, foxing, and it made her all the more keen to annihilate him. She would not get annoyed, because that would prejudice her chance of winning.

They played in complete silence, with total concentration, and the tension built up higher and higher. Each one was determined to win and each one knowing there was more at stake than a mere game. It was very even, piece for piece, attack then defence, defence then attack. After an hour they still had an equal number of pieces on the board and Shannon knew that it would take a miracle for her to beat him, but she thought she could hold him to a draw.

Suddenly she saw a way to sacrifice her queen, and be able to have checkmate two moves later. She couldn't believe her luck. She brushed aside her hair, as if losing concentration, then moved her bishop, leaving her queen exposed to his rook. Would James take the bait? Was it too obvious? She held her breath, knowing he wouldn't be able to resist it, but oh, he was cautious. Then he snapped it up and she made her second move.

'Check!' she cried in triumph.

James sat back, and eyed the board disbelievingly. That move she had made obviously puzzled him, then he saw it and with a flourish resigned, laying his king down. 'Congratulations—a fine game. I don't know when I've been so stretched.'

With sparkling eyes, Shannon admitted her move

was a sheer fluke. 'A chance in a million. I thought you weren't going to take it—I nearly expired!'

For the first time she saw real respect in his eyes.

'I should have seen it,' he admitted. 'I should have known you wouldn't make a careless move after the way you've been playing, but we all have sudden loss of concentration at times. Shall I set them up again?'

'No, thank you. I'll quit while I'm ahead. I think Joshua's grizzling. I'll give him a bottle, and change his pants. Goodnight.'

He carefully packed the pieces away, saying wearily, 'Did you want to play golf with Brad tomorrow?'

'Not really.' She moved across from the sink so that she could see him.

'Good. Goodnight, then.'

Shannon attended to Joshua, then went to bed. That game of chess had cleared her mind, blotted out all the crazy thoughts she had been having. Shannon snuggled down under the blankets. It was beautiful to think that it might be like teething— some got it bad, some got off lightly. Perhaps hers was only a temporary aberration. In fact, she was positive . . . just a passing fancy.

She fell asleep.

Joshua was yelling his head off when she struggled awake, and she grabbed her robe and in a daze hurried to him. Lifting him out of the cot, she carried him to the kitchen. He was really upset, and she didn't want him waking Marigold. One-handed she filled his bottle, and took him on her knee, but he pushed the bottle away, screaming. She tried to comfort him, but he was inconsolable, then without warning he vomited. 'Ah, you poor wee love. There, there!'

'Can I help?' James was beside her.

'He's all messy. I'll strip him off, then wrap him in a cuddly. Then you can hold him while I get us both some fresh gear.' She quickly sponged the wee boy clean, then gave him to James. Shivering in her room, she grabbed a fresh nightgown, flung on a brunchcoat, and hurried back with clean baby clothes. And Joshua was promptly sick again.

And she dressed him again. 'Oh, I don't know what to do to help him, poor baby. Brad said there wasn't a lot we could do really.'

'I'll light the stove again. At least he'll be warm. There's a really beaut frost tonight. It's three o'clock, so it's not long till morning, and we'll have some medicine for him.'

While James lit the stove, Shannon walked up and down the room, trying to comfort Joshua, trying to interest him in a bottle, or a biscuit, or a toy, but nothing pleased him. He didn't want to be nursed, he didn't want to be put down.

'Here, give him to me.' James tightened the belt of his robe and then took the baby, but he was equally unsuccessful. After an hour they were both feeling helpless and exhausted.

Then Joshua stopped crying and fell asleep, and Shannon put him back in his cot.

'Here's your cup of tea, you didn't get a chance to drink it. I'll be off while the going's good,' James said, emptying a bucket of coal into the stove. 'This will keep going till morning now, in case he gets up again.'

Shannon sipped her tea wearily. 'Brad says he could go on like that for three weeks.'

'I hope not—that pain must be murder. He's a tough kid, and rarely cries. 'Night.'

' 'Night.' She finished her tea, and crept back to bed. It hardly seemed that she had closed her eyes when Joshua was yelling again. She flew out of bed and carried him to the kitchen, ready for him to be sick, but he wasn't. He just whimpered and moaned, half awake, half asleep. She glanced at the clock—only five o'clock. The night was endless. Joshua was sick once more, but only her brunchcoat copped it, so she stripped it off, leaving her in the dreadful 'joke' nightshirt that Trisha had given her, but it was warm sitting by the stove. Each time he cried she rocked him back to a restless sleep. She had put the light off and was content with the glow from the fire. The light seemed to bother Joshua.

She dozed, off and on, then suddenly the light came on and she blinked against the glare. 'James, is that you?'

'Who were you expecting? Have you been sitting here all night? Why didn't you call me?'

Painfully Shannon moved her cramped muscles, and stood up. 'There was no point in us both being up. And he really wasn't so bad, just making a sad wee hurt noise, but he'd wake and yell each time I put him down, so it was easier just to rock him now and again.'

'I'll stoke the stove and get a cuppa on. He looks sound asleep now, why don't you try putting him down again, and grab a bit more sleep yourself? I'll hang about and pick him up if he cries.'

'What a lovely thought!' Shannon carefully laid Joshua down, covered him and crept out. She stood by the table waiting for James to turn round before saying, 'You're sure it won't keep you from your work? I *could* carry on.'

He stepped closer to her with a broad grin on his face. 'I can see that, but I didn't expect it of you, really.'

Shannon looked at him blankly. 'What are you talking about?'

'Do you think it pays to advertise?' James stretched out his hand and lightly ran a finger across the embroidery which was stitched on her breast, and laughed.

At his touch Shannon jumped back, feeling that crazy liquid fire pounce on her again and sear through her whole body. She glanced down and remembered her 'joke' nightshirt. Some joke! Stretched prominently over her thrusting breasts were written, 'Please make love to me', and 'Climb every mountain'. Scarlet, she knew James had been reading the rest of the more blatantly encouraging messages, placed very strategically in more important places. On each buttock were stitched men's hands curved impudently, and the challenge, 'Try me, I could be your size'—and she had turned her back to take Joshua to his room, and she would have to do it again to get to her own.

'Why don't you take a cold shower!' she yelled furiously. 'I only put it on because Joshua was sick on my others. It was a present from Trisha. It keeps me warm, anyway!'

She whirled and headed to her room, and heard him roar laughing again. 'That nightshirt would make any man warm as well!'

Shannon slammed the door behind her. Sleep had disappeared from her programme completely. Oh, she wished she had Trisha here—she would kill her slowly and painfully without mercy. It had been only a fun thing, just as she was preparing her honeymoon case. She'd said, 'This is yours, Shannon, you're so sexually inexperienced and backward that any guy who gets you into bed will need a lot of encouragement.'

They had all laughed when she had tried it on. It was in a clingy knit material, a size too small, and very provocative. Worse than being stark naked, it over-emphasised everything.

She stripped it off and walked to the mirror, examining her body for defects. Thank goodness she didn't have an extra ounce on her well-shaped body

. . . it would have shown. Tentatively, she touched the rise of her breast, where James' finger had rested, and again was swamped with an emotional explosion. It had not gone away, that frightening, almost wonderful, mysterious longing. Quickly she dressed in jeans and skivvy and a bulky cardigan. Her body didn't even feel like her own . . . it was strange and new.

Why had this flowering of sexual awareness been delayed so long? And was it more potent because of the delay? She had always been so condemning of girls who had to rush into marriage because of an unexpected pregnancy, saying sadly, 'I couldn't help myself. I loved him too much to say no.'

She had been so self-righteous and smug, she had not known this desire, this demanding urgency before. She had never wanted a man before . . . how could she have judged them? This was a hunger within that appalled her by its intensity, and she didn't even love the man who made her feel this way.

Whenever she had thought of marriage, she had wondered a little at her disinclination for the whole thing, but had put it down to her planned travel scheme. And it had been nothing of the sort. She had just been immature, unawakened. She still did not approve of sex before marriage, but she had to admit it was a force to be reckoned with. She had told James to take a cold shower, perhaps she should take her own advice. She remembered scoffing at those magazine articles, 'Sex and the single woman'. She wished she could lay her hands on an encyclopaedia about the subject.

With heightened colour she went out to the kitchen.

'Sorry about yelling at you. I deserved your remarks for wearing that idiotic shirt.'

'I found it very attractive,' James said slyly, then grinned.

Shannon laughed. He knew how to needle back when he got the chance, but she *had* beaten him at chess.

She popped the toast into the toaster and poured herself a cup of tea, her senses screamingly aware of him sitting beside her, his checked shirt open at the throat, his strong-muscled arm near her, his long jean-clad legs inches away from her own. Grimly she thought he'd be blushing if he could read her thoughts. Oh, Mighty McCabe, you're a menace, she thought, but I'll never let you have the satisfaction of knowing into what turmoil you've thrown my nice, controlled life.

You'll never know, my gorgeous hunk of man, that I find you almost irresistible. Brad and his psychology would be beaten and perish. She just had to put her mind to it.

CHAPTER SIX

JAMES seemed reluctant to leave, even after he had finished his breakfast. Maybe he was tired after being up with Joshua. Maybe the potbellied stove was very attractive considering the crisp white frost Shannon saw out of the window.

He sat with his long legs resting on the wire guard which ran around the stove for safety, balancing his chair precariously on two legs. She would have loved to know what he was thinking. He followed her every move with a curious speculative gleam in his blue eyes. The scrutiny was a bit unnerving, but she ignored him, concentrating on dressing Marigold and giving her her breakfast and washing the dishes.

Maybe he was re-living his defeat at chess. He really had been magnificent in defeat. She could not have conceded defeat so gracefully. Maybe they taught a course on good sportsmanship at whatever posh boarding school he had attended.

Almost as if he'd read her mind he asked, 'Where did you learn to play chess?'

'Oh, William almost lived his chess. He would sit in the evenings, either playing or thinking of games. We used to tease him. You could tell by his expression whether he was winning the game he was playing in his mind, or losing. He'd frown furiously, or burst into an unnerving chuckle. He plays in the Northern Championships and is highly graded.'

'And he taught you?' James asked, obviously interested.

'Well, his own girls hated chess and he had to have someone to practice on, so there was only me.

He started teaching me when I was about twelve. He took it seriously, and expected me to also. I got madly keen for a while at college, went in for tournaments—you know, time clock, the whole works, but lately I just play when he can't find a better opponent.' She finished the dishes.

'He'd be hard put to it to do that. You play a mean game.' There was real respect in his voice.

'Oh, I'm not just a pretty face,' Shannon said with a laugh, but she was enormously pleased with the compliment.

'You're not,' James agreed with a smile, then swung his stockinged feet off the guard and stood up. 'As you told Brad, and I've learned by experience, you've got hidden talents.'

She spun around and aimed a sodden dischloth at him, but he dodged and went out the back door. She didn't have to ask what he was referring to ... that wretched nightshirt. Things were looking up!

'You threw a dishcloth at James,' Marigold said in very disapproving tones.

'I did, and he deserved it. With a little practice I'll score a hit next time.'

Marigold's almond-shaped eyes lit up with excitement, 'Can I have a go, too?'

Shannon shook her head, 'No, it's a game only grown-ups can play. What would you like to do while Joshua's asleep? How about playdough, or painting?'

'I'd like to paint, please.'

Shannon quickly set the things out on the table.

'I've got heaps of washing to do. Thank goodness for an automatic washing machine. Call me if you hear Joshua. He's been crying all night with his teeth, so he'll probably stay asleep.'

She had only put the first load in when Marigold called her, and she lifted a very grumpy boy from his cot. He swacked at his bottle, knocked his porridge to the floor, pulled Marigold's hair when she went to console him. As soon as he was put on the floor he went to the bookcase and pulled out the books one by one, throwing them over his shoulder. Shannon decided to ignore it, although he had been taught not to touch them. Noticing that she was not upset, he turned and started to rip the pages.

'Naughty! You must not do that, Joshua!' Shannon rushed to rescue James' valuable books.

That did it. Joshua collapsed in brokenhearted sobs, and nothing she did could cheer him up. She felt such a brute for having scolded him when he wasn't well. She carried him with her to the washhouse, to the bedroom, but found it difficult to do anything properly, as his cries went on and on. Desperate, she walked and rocked him, wishing the bus would come, but it wasn't due for another hour.

James came in and put a parcel on the table. 'Thought I'd go in and get the stuff from Brad, but I had to wait till the chemist opened.'

'Oh, James, you're fantastic!' Gratitude shone in her eyes. So that was why he'd been hanging around instead of going to work. He really was thoughtful.

'There's this stuff. You rub it on his gums. It's like anaesthetic, kills the pain.' He handed her the tube.

'Whew! That's exactly what we need.' She applied it to the two angry-looking eruptions on Joshua's lower gum, and waited hopefully for the tears to dry, but the tired wailing went on and on.

'What shall we do?' she appealed frantically to James. 'It's not working. Have you anything else?'

'Just this, but you're not supposed to over-use it. Sparingly, Brad said, to put him out at nights.' He looked at her pale tired face. 'Get the kids' windbreakers on and put their gumboots on, you're all coming with me to move the cattle. It's cold, but the sun is up, and the air is like wine. Chilled, of course. Get well wrapped up, yourself. A walk will do you good. Brad said you needed taking out of the house. I got one of those backpack contraptions while I was in town.'

Marigold was wildly excited, and Joshua stopped crying and beamed as Shannon pulled on his padded jacket and hood. Shannon was excited too. Walking with James, seeing his farm, would be a new experience. Like loving him.

With Joshua comfortably settled on his back, James led the way, with his dogs, Scot and Jade, at his heels and Marigold dancing and whirling beside him like a colourful spinning top. Shannon walked a pace or two behind, fascinated by the beauty about her. The manuka was frosted like an English Christmas card, each twig and branch pristine white, and each blade of grass was frozen perfection, even the cobwebs on the fences were like beaded diamonds, flashing and scintillating in the bright sunlight. A flock of large birds flew overhead with rapid wing movement, calling raucously.

'What are they, James?'

'Plovers. Seagulls over there, and see, in the next paddock—magpies.' He held the gate open, letting the dogs and Marigold through and waiting for Shannon. 'Do you like birds?'

Her eyes were shining. 'I don't know. I think so. It's as if I'd never noticed them before I came here. There's a blackbird that sings his heart out in the tree by my window each morning. I think that's what started me off. And the wekas in the hedge. Then there's the tuis in the old plum tree when I'm hanging out the washing, and pigeons in the fir trees where we got the cones. Oh, James, what are *they*? Aren't they marvellous!'

He grinned, knowing that she hadn't even noticed

she was clutching his arm in her enthusiasm. 'Paradise ducks, and you'll see them everywhere at this time of year. They'll be in pairs. It's nearly nesting season and they're picking their mates.'

Shannon said softly, under her breath, 'Half their luck.'

'Paradise duck,' he repeated, thinking she had not heard correctly.

'Let him go, Shannon. I want to see the cattle,' Marigold called shrilly.

Shannon stepped away as if burned. 'Sorry, I guess I got a bit excited. Oh, I love this place, just the wee bit I know around the house, those palm trees out front, and the old arbour that's falling down. It must be a sight in the summer, covered with roses and honeysuckle. And even though the garden's neglected, I can see rose beds, and dahlia beds and chrysanthemums . . . someone must have really cared for it once.'

'Move,' James said curtly. He slammed the gate shut, and went striding away so fast she had to almost run to keep up. She really had upset him, and for once she was genuinely sorry. She followed them through another gateway, then saw about a hundred cattle held within a two-string fence, heads up waiting for him, roaring occasionally with a mournful note.

'Marigold, Shannon,' he said sternly, making sure he had their full attention, 'all the fences here are electrified. If you touch a fence you'll get a whale of a jolt. It will hurt you and scare you. I know the ones which are carrying power, so don't climb through unless you see me do it. Do you understand?'

They both nodded vigorously.

'Are you sure now, Marigold? What did I say?'

'Not to touch the fences. Not to climb on them unless you do.'

'Good. Why not?'

' 'Cos they're 'lectric, and will kill us.'

'Not quite, but close.' James smiled down at her small, earnest face. 'I'll keep you on. You always listen when I speak.'

'Joshua's gone to sleep,' Shannon observed quietly. She did not want to upset James again. She'd hate to be sent home. If only she could win his unqualified approval as easily as Marigold did!

'Great, I thought he might. With luck he'll sleep all the way round. Come on, we'll shift the calves.'

'Calves?' Shannon repeated incredulously. 'They're more like elephants!'

James stepped over the double string fence. 'Come on, they won't hurt you.'

Marigold eyed him suspiciously. 'That fence might bite me.'

'No, it won't. I took the fuse out at the gate. I told you if I climb a fence you can.'

Marigold took his hand and Shannon walked nearly on his heels through the cattle to the second fence. Calves, huh! These big things weren't lovely small calves as in picture books.

James made an opening and the calves poured through on to the new strip of long green grass, starting to eat greedily. The piece they had left was almost chewed bare.

'Now we move that fence and put it ahead of them ready for tomorrow. You two can help.'

Half an hour later they walked back to the gate and he replaced the fuse. 'That's called block grazing, a method of intensive farming. I can carry double the young stock by this method. Enjoy yourself, Marigold?'

'Oh, yes—can I come every day?'

'I don't see why not. I'll rearrange my schedule to suit you.'

'I love you,' smiled Marigold, hugging his legs

just above his gumboots, which was as high as she could reach.

'It's mutual,' he told her. 'Now, Shannon, what do you think? You can go back across these two paddocks to the house, or you can come round the sheep if you're not too tired.'

'I'm not tired. I'm loving it.'

'I think Marigold will make it, although it's a fair step. There's a bird you don't know. They're welcome swallows, my favourites. They have the split swallow tail, but are small like fantails. They fly in erratic, swooping flight patterns.'

'They're blue, a fantastic deep blue,' Shannon noticed. 'How lovely! Welcome swallow—that's a nice name.'

Wherever they walked there were pairs of Paradise ducks, their iridescent feathers gleaming green and blue and black and red, and when they flew overhead their white wing feathers flashed. Shannon felt they were flaunting their togetherness, male and female, brilliantly beautiful, honking and trumpeting their superiority over her singleness.

Being in love appeared to have made her see beauty with a new clarity. The gnarled bark on the trees, the tiny brown creek they crossed, the green upon green of the native trees, the golden gorse flower, exquisite ferns and rushing miniature waterfalls in the bush ... each was a work of art to be held in the heart.

They moved the sheep, then the larger cattle, and the sun was warm on their backs, the frost all gone.

'Home it is. You've done well, Marigold—you too, Shannon, for a townie. Not bad,' James told them.

'You've forgotten the mad bull,' Shannon felt forced to say, while still accepting his praise gratefully.

'You won't forget it, and it wasn't a mad bull, it was a perfectly harmless two-year-old steer, with a keen natural interest in strangers.'

Shannon smiled. He was right, she'd never forget it. She had been standing by James, a bit nervously watching the cattle edging closer and closer in a half circle, when she felt something nudge the middle of her back, and had looked around straight into the face of a huge white-faced Hereford bull, steer, whatever. She had screamed and flung herself on James, almost climbing up his body in her panic. The animal bellowed, James said in fright, and she had clung so tightly she nearly strangled him. She wished she'd completed the job when he laughed heartlessly. She was still a bit shaky, but wasn't sure if it was from contact with James or with the bull, steer, or whatever.

'Put the kettle on while I tie up the dogs, I'll have to move to get up to Gary,' he ordered.

'Gary?' she queried.

'I told you, I have to look at a farm with my cousin, and I'm late.'

'Oh, I'd forgotten.' Disappointment was in her wide brown eyes. 'We've had such a wonderful time I was planning a special lunch as a reward for you.'

'I'll be in for dinner. More time to plan.'

Shannon walked towards the house, feeling like a bottle of champagne which had been shaken hard. Fantastic, unless someone took the top off.

After he left she felt flatter than a pancake. If she felt like this after being in love only one day, what would it be like when she'd been in love a whole week, or a whole month? She was sitting at the table, her head propped in her hands, staring bemused out the window. Then the awful fact hit her. When she had been in love a month, she wouldn't even be here. She wouldn't be seeing James every day, she wouldn't be cooking him fancy meals, she wouldn't be making his bed and doing his washing and ironing.

It was a horrible thought. What was the matter with her? One moment she was determined to extinguish this storm inside her, then the next moment she wanted it to continue for ever. The children were playing on the verandah. The walk had lifted them all up. Even Joshua had enjoyed his lunch and forgotten his new tooth.

A knock at the door brought her upright. She walked jauntily through the lounge to the front door, and opened it.

A tall, slender woman with carefully styled blue-rinsed hair stood there with a nervous look on her face.

'Is Mr McCabe at home?'

'No, I'm sorry, he's away—probably won't be back until about six.'

'Oh, dear, I did want to see him. I haven't been in these parts for years, and I'm just passing through.'

There was something odd about her, Shannon thought. Certainly not her clothes, they were most fashionable. She was waiting for . . . what?

'I'd like to come in for a minute if I may. I used to stay here a lot.'

'Oh, I'm sorry.' Shannon stepped away from the door. 'Would you like a cup of tea, or coffee?'

'Tea would be lovely.' She followed Shannon out to the kitchen, her eyes restlessly travelling over the walls, the floors, the furniture.

Shannon put the kettle on. She was worried. James would murder her for inviting this woman in. But she hadn't really; it was more of a self-invitation. But he was almost paranoid about his private affairs, and how could she fend off questions from an old family friend, without appearing rude? He'd told his relatives to keep away.

Sighing, she put out the cups and saucers and a plate of biscuits. The woman was sitting quietly with hands clasped, her mind obviously miles away. She had a strong face, a bit thin, deep dark-shadowed eyes and an almost sad expression in repose. Shannon handed her the tea, wondering who the lady reminded her of. There was something familiar.

'I was a friend of James' mother,' she volunteered. 'Do you know her?'

Shannon shook her head. 'No, I'm sorry, I don't.'

'Are you a relative?'

'No.' This was getting awkward.

'I am stupid—you'll be James' wife,' the woman exclaimed.

'No, I'm not,' Shannon answered pleasantly. Now we come to the six-million-dollar question.

'I do apologise. My name is McCabe too. What's yours?'

'Shannon Haldane.'

'That's a very pretty name,' she smiled, and the smile transformed her face.

She looked like James, Shannon thought in amazement. She must be a very close relative. This was getting more awkward by the minute. There was a yowl from the verandah and thankfully Shannon rushed out to the children, flinging an apology over her shoulder.

'He pulled my doll out of the bassinette, and I tried to stop him and felled over. I *didn't* hit him.'

'How *very* restrained. You're a good girl. I'll take him inside with me and then he won't annoy you. Do you want a biscuit?'

'No, thanks. I'm busy.'

Shannon smiled as she closed the outside door. Would the baby help the conversation, or just cause more questions?

'This is Joshua,' she told the visitor. 'He's teething.'

The effect on the woman was quite remarkable. Her face went snowy white, and Shannon thought she was going to faint.

'Whose child is that?'

'This is James' nephew. His father was Mark McCabe. He died last year.'

'I know, I know.' It was the merest whisper. 'Could I ... could I hold him for a moment, please?'

'Yes, but he's mighty heavy. Are you sure you can manage?'

'I'll manage.' Her voice was stronger. She took Joshua very carefully into her arms, and to Shannon's horror started to cry in harsh sobs. Joshua peered interestedly at her, then laid his smooth face against her wet, wrinkled cheek. 'Aaah!'

Slowly the woman controlled herself, and held him away so that she could see him better. 'He's the image of Mark, the very image.'

Shannon stood close by, troubled and uncertain. What should she do? She wished James was at home. He always knew what to do.

Making up her mind, she went through to the lounge and brought back a glass of sherry. 'Do drink this, you need something a little stronger than tea.' She lifted Joshua down and gave him a tin with blocks to play with. 'He's very big for his age.'

'He's not fat at all!' Mrs McCabe said defensively.

Shannon smiled, 'I didn't mean that. He's all bone and muscle, built like an All-Black.'

Mrs McCabe sipped her sherry, all the while her eyes fastened on the baby. Slowly her colour returned.

'I suppose you know all about this family.' There was defeat in her voice.

'I know nothing about the McCabe family,' Shannon assured her. 'I've only met James, and he's the original clam.'

'But you go into town? I'm sure there were plenty there only too willing to give you the background,' she said bitterly.

'James warned me to give no information away, and to listen to none.'

'And you do everything he asks you? What is James to you?'

'My employer,' Shannon said very carefully. 'He pays me, and has my loyalty. I really don't think I should answer any more of your questions. Could you possibly call back this evening? James may tell you all you want to know.'

'James would order me off the place. He's hard and unforgiving.' The woman started to cry again, deep harsh crying that shook her whole body, her hands covering her face.

Shannon sat quietly, completely out of her depth.

Marigold came and stood, hands behind her back, staring. 'What's she crying for? Did she hurt herself?'

'Yes. Mrs McCabe, this is Marigold, Mark's daughter.' A suspicion was forming in her mind.

The woman dropped her hands and stared at Marigold.

'She must be like her mother—there's nothing of Mark there. Come here, child.'

Marigold gave her a wary look and shot round the table to lean against Shannon. 'No!'

The woman sighed, 'I'm sorry, I didn't mean to frighten you.' She looked directly across at Shannon. 'I should have been honest. I'm Andrew McCabe's wife, mother of James and Mark, and Louise. I'm the children's grandmother, and I didn't even know they existed. You've no idea how painful this is for me . . . to come here. By chance a friend was passing through here and said she saw two children playing in the garden, and presumed James had married. I just wanted to see the children and, I thought, his wife . . . just to know that one of us had found happiness. I was just going to pretend to be a visitor, come and look and leave. It wasn't too much to want.'

The pain in her hurt Shannon and she said gruffly, 'You don't owe me any explanation, Mrs McCabe. What if James had been home?'

'I asked young Gary to get him away for the afternoon. They knew nothing of what was happening here, only gossip and rumours. But when I saw Mark's baby. . . .' She stopped, unable to go on for a minute. 'You said his name was Joshua.'

Joshua, hearing his name, looked around with a sparkling-eyed smile and crawled rapidly towards her. She lifted him up and in her eyes were the same intense yearning and longing that had been in James' eyes the first time he met Joshua.

Shannon blessed the fact that Joshua had no shyness whatsoever. He was busy trying to detach an expensive brooch from his grandmother's lapel. Marigold was cautiously edging around the table like a wary bird, alert for danger. Shannon pushed a book across to her.

'Perhaps your grandmother will read you a story. I'll just prepare the meat for dinner.'

Mrs McCabe looked up. 'I have as much right to these children as James. Has he adopted them? Where's their mother?'

'I won't discuss James or his plans with you,' said Shannon. 'I really don't want to be rude to you, I can see you're far from well, but I ask you again to get in touch with James yourself. He's a hard man, but he's been very kind to these children. You're putting me in a very awkward position. Why don't you just enjoy the children for a while?'

'I'll do that. I'm sorry I pressured you, it's not your quarrel.'

With relief Shannon heard her making overtures to Marigold, then reading a story. While she busied herself preparing the dinner she wondered how James would react to the situation. She wished that she didn't need to tell him, but Marigold would. Still, as Mrs McCabe had said, it wasn't her problem . . . well, it wasn't unless if affected Michelle and the children, then they'd better watch it.

When Joshua started to become grizzly, she prepared his bottle, put fresh nappies on and put him down. He fell asleep immediately and the relief was enormous. Marigold went back to her dolls on the verandah and Shannon was again alone with Mrs McCabe.

'Do you know their mother?' The tone was softer, all anger gone.

'Yes, I do.'

'What's she like?'

'Very, very beautiful. One of the most gentle, loving girls I've ever met. She loved Mark very deeply and is still grieving.'

'Yet she let James have the children?'

'She's been ill. It hasn't been easy for her.'

'Where is she? Could you give me her address? I would like to visit her, help her if I could.'

Shannon stared out of the window. The woman sounded sincere. Michelle could certainly use some help, but was it help? Perhaps it would just leave Michelle caught in between two strong, determined people, another tug-of-war, with the children as the prize. Yet, could she deny Michelle this offer?

'I don't know what to say. Would you be prepared to leave your address with me? If Michelle wants to see you, she'll write to you.'

'If James permits it?' Mrs McCabe said angrily. 'And he won't ever forgive me.'

'I don't know about that,' Shannon said patiently. 'But you can trust me to talk to Michelle. It's her decision, not one for James or me.'

Mrs McCabe stood up. 'You've been very kind, and fair. Here's my card, and I truly appreciate your giving me a slim chance to regain my self-respect. Would you tell Mark's wife that I tried to get in touch with her when Mark died? . . . I didn't hear for weeks afterwards, and she'd moved. I should have made a greater effort, but I thought Mark would have set her against me, too. I didn't mean to destroy the family, but life was unbearable and I left. It seemed the only way out for me.'

Shannon saw the tortured expression and longed to offer a crumb of comfort. 'Michelle has no animosity towards the McCabes, nor to her own family. She has also survived a situation which most people would consider unbearable, and if you met I think you'd be friends.' She walked to the gate with her.

'Thank you again, Shannon. We may not ever meet again, but I shan't forget you. To come back to this house, to look at the garden I loved, neglected and overgrown, and to expect to find the house cold and unwelcoming. . . . Yet, because you were here, I'll remember this as a happy time. You offered me hospitality, you let me get to know the children, you didn't condemn me, and I didn't deserve any of these courtesies.'

Shannon smiled at her. 'It could all work out . . . don't give up hope.'

'I have no hope, unless perhaps you're going to marry James?'

Shannon laughed outright. 'No chance! He's against marriage, and usually against me. He considers me an interfering female.'

'And you?'

'Oh, marriage is not on my agenda either.' It wasn't the thought of marriage that sent that warm glow racing through her veins, melting her heart like hot sun on a frost.

'So James will never live in the house on Blue Ridge. Does anyone live there?'

Shannon followed the direction of Mrs McCabe's gaze and saw her staring at the modern farmhouse, beautifully situated among the native bush high on a plateau some distance away. 'Is that part of this farm too?' she asked.

'Yes. James built that five years ago when he was going to marry Sandra. I was foolish to think he would recover from that. The pity of it all—an empty house, and an empty man. Will you tell him I called?'

'Marigold will. She's never had a grandmother before.'

Mrs McCabe fought back her tears. 'Tell him I was wrong, and I'm sorry.' She hurried round to the driver's door of an expensive-looking car and got in and drove off without looking back.

Shannon leaned against the gate, looking up at the house. She'd thought it was a near neighbour, but it was James' house. So he had once loved someone enough to build her a house on Blue Ridge. A shaft of sunlight from the setting sun touched the house, giving it an almost dreamlike appearance. Poor James, to have loved so well and lost so much, and to see a permanent reminder every day ... 'You'll be my breath when I grow old' ... that's loving. Would she still remember five years from now? She thought she would. It didn't help much. Empty man, empty house, and herself, empty heart.

She was glad he was late home. She wanted time

to prepare the special dinner. The children had been bathed and fed and she hoped to get Marigold settled before he came in.

He was in such a good humour. It lasted scarcely five minutes, until Marigold shattered it.

'I've got a grandmother,' she announced importantly, just as he was hearing her prayers. 'Can I say, God bless Grandmother?'

'Yes, that would be kind.'

'She read me a story, my grandmother.'

'Finish your prayers.' James shot a sharp glance at Shannon. She continued to tuck Joshua down, adding a little prayer of her own that the medicine would work. It had been a long day, and that flicking muscle in James' cheek made the special dinner seem wasted.

'What was Marigold going on about?' he asked. 'Were some of Michelle's relatives here? I told you that they were to have no contact with the children.'

'Could we leave this until after dinner, please, James? I'm so tired. I don't want a yelling match until after I've eaten.' It probably wasn't the most tactful way that she could have framed the request.

'We will not leave it.' His eyes were flintlike, his face set like granite. 'I leave you one day—well, a couple of hours, and you deliberately go against me. You're completely untrustworthy!'

'Okay, just give me a minute and I'll answer all your questions.' She was trying to postpone the anger and the fury he would pour over her, just to prolong for an hour the lightness in their relationship that had come about from the game of chess, from sharing little Joshua's misery last night, the teasing about the nightshirt, the walk this morning. Only little things, but they were like tiny stepping-stones leading across a torrent of mistrust and suspicion. If

James would only give them time they might make a whole bridge.

She flew to the refrigerator, and placed in the centre of the table the most fabulous pavlova she had ever made, swirling with whipped cream, decorated with luscious peaches. Then to the oven, lifting out a crown roast, a triumph of her culinary art. Didn't he even notice that the silver and crystal were polished and shining, that she had set the table with love? It looked beautiful, with a red berry and green fir decoration. Didn't he notice that she was wearing a gauzy blouse, and that her hair was washed and shining like the wings of the welcome swallow?

She faced him, silently pleading with him not to destroy all her efforts to please . . . not just yet, her brown eyes entreated, her smile a little unsure. 'Could we eat first, please, James?'

'No!' he thundered, standing exactly where she had left him, dark with rage. 'Why did you let them in?'

Her expression changed, and the softness left her voice. 'Because I didn't finish my course in karate. Because I'm hired to mind the children, not to be a bouncer. Because I was brought up not to hit little old ladies. Do you want any more reasons?'

'They're scum, the lowest of the low, and you opened my house to them. Have you no loyalty? They lured young Mark away, severed his ties with his family, and are virtually responsible for his death, and I will not have them leeching on to me via the kids!'

Shannon's eyes narrowed dangerously. 'It was *your* mother,' she flung at him. 'She described herself as the wife of Andrew McCabe, mother of James, and Mark, and Louise—no identity for herself except through you lot. Your mother, James, who carried

you nine months in her body, who changed your
nappies, who fed you, who wiped your runny nose,
who walked the floor with you when you were
teething, who loved you and cherished you . . . and
now had to pretend to be a stranger to get a look at
what she thought were your wife and children!'

She knew her temper had got away on her, but
she couldn't stop. Staring at his second shirt button
because she dared not meet his eyes, she carried on.
'I don't know what happened in this family, except
that you've all destroyed yourselves with bitterness.
She looked nice to me, sad and kind of helpless. Yes,
I let her see the children, let her hold them, let her
play with them for a while. I gave her a cup of tea,
I gave her a sherry too, because I thought she was
going to pass out on me when she saw Joshua. She
came apart, just the way you did when you saw how
like Mark he was. And she thanked me, she thought
I was kind, because I didn't condemn her. She must
have had plenty of that, to be so grateful for a
stranger treating her with ordinary human kindness!'

The tears were pouring down her face, but she
didn't even bother to wipe them away. This was the
end, she would take the children and leave in the
morning, but the words still rushed out of her like
flood waters through a broken dam. 'She said you
were hard and unforgiving, and she was right.
You're so damn perfect that you don't give anyone a
chance! We all make mistakes, and if we get love we
can recover . . . but you don't know what the word
means. You're empty like the empty house on Blue
Ridge, nursing your hurt, gloating over your griev-
ances. . . .'

'Are you nearly finished?' His tone would have
scared her, if she hadn't been beyond fear.

'No! She said she only came to see if you had

found happiness. She wanted that for you. She loved
Mark, she loved those children, and she still loves
you. She left a message, to tell you that she was
wrong and that she was sorry. I have her address.
I'm going to give it to Michelle, and she can decide
whether she wants to see her or not . . . and I think
she will. I *was* loyal to you. I refused to discuss you
or your business. I wouldn't let her tell me what
happened to this family that once had everything
and now has nothing but money. I wish I'd listened,
then I might understand why you hate Michelle,
why Mark died, why your mother looks so desperate,
and why you, who could be so fine, are so . . . so
empty!'

'I'll tell you if you like.' His voice was cold, completely without emotion.

'I don't want to hear!' She shouted. 'I cooked you
a lovely dinner, but you wouldn't share it with me.
You can eat it on your own. And you can wash up
too. I'm going to bed, and in the morning I'll leave,
and I'll take the children with me. If you think I'd
leave them for you to bring up you're wrong! You
have iron in your soul, and I won't let those loving
children grow up to be hard like you!'

She tried to pass him to go to her room, but he
put his hands on her shoulders. 'You talk too much.'
He didn't sound angry, just tired. 'Perhaps I should
have explained it to you, but I've never been able to
talk about it to anyone. Will you listen?'

'No! I don't want to hear.' Something in his voice
warned her that it was horrible . . . more than she
could bear.

His fingers bit into her flesh through the flimsy
blouse. 'You've listened to everyone else, you can
now hear me out. I was engaged to Sandra. I
brought her home here. I built that house on the
hill. You were right to believe we had everything

. . . our family was special, until she came into it. She was a very beautiful girl, exciting and unusual and completely unprincipled. She seduced my father . . . my mother found them. She blamed me for introducing her into the family. She left this house and never spoke to any of us again except through a solicitor. She took half the farm, which was her legal right. My father was an upright and honest man all his life and he was filled with remorse, humiliated and without dignity before his children. He tried to hold things together, but Mark ran wild, then Louise. . . .'

Shannon was still crying, but softly now. She wanted him to stop. She didn't want to hear any more, but in the same dead flat voice he continued.

'My father made what was left of the farm over to me. There wasn't enough left to keep us both, and I've had to work like hell to hold what I had. He took a position with the Wool Board and is in America now. You're right, saying everyone makes mistakes, but at least he tried to put his right.' His hands dropped. 'I won't let you take the children away. You agreed to six weeks, you'll keep to that agreement. Do you want dinner now?'

'I'm not hungry.' Shannon walked to her room. She couldn't even think straight, she was absolutely drained. She had said such terrible things to James, and she had not understood anything. She was worse than him. She had judged him and condemned him, and nothing would ever be right between them again. She was too tired to think at all . . . but she loved him. He had not asked for her sympathy, yet he deserved it most. He had loved Sandra, and she betrayed him . . . with his own father. What would that do to a young man?

She crawled into bed. She wanted to go out and say she was sorry, but it was useless. She wanted to put her arms around him and comfort him, but he wouldn't let her do that, he was too proud. She had jeered at him, poured scorn on him, called him hard and unforgiving, yet he must have suffered more than them all. It was his love that had been rejected, his girl, whom he introduced into the family, who had torn them all apart. Now she could understand why he wanted the children, to shelter and protect them and to provide for them . . . to start rebuilding a small remnant of the family he had once had.

She could even understand a little of his hardness against Michelle. He was wrong, of course he was wrong, but women had not given him any reason to put his trust in them. Oh, she wished she had held her tongue, but you couldn't go back. How could she face him in the morning? She buried her face in the pillow and cried herself to sleep.

CHAPTER SEVEN

SHANNON was woken by the blackbird in the tree outside her window. She sat up and rubbed her eyes. It must be very late, the sun was already up, shining brightly on a world transformed with the white magic of frost. Her heart lifted in response to the glorious rhapsody pouring from the bird's throat. She flipped back the blankets and the memory of the night before rushed at her, but strangely did not alter her mood. Against all reason she felt ridiculously happy. She picked up her robe and towel, hoping there would be time for a shower before the children woke.

The hot water banished any lingering doubts that her sense of happiness was only temporary, and she sang as she soaped herself, feeling a new exhilaration. All she could think of was that, in spite of her behaviour, James had wanted her to stay. For sure it was only for the sake of the children, but whatever the reason, she had four more weeks in his company.

When she returned through the kitchen, aglow with the vigorous towelling she had given herself, she found James stoking the stove.

'Good morning, James, another frost.' Pretend nothing had happened, oh, James, pretend like I am.

'Good morning, Shannon,' he answered politely, looking at her vivacious face, his expression unreadable. 'I've had my breakfast. I'll do a few odd jobs while you get the children dressed and fed, then you can come with me round the stock, if you want to.'

'Oh, James!' she exclaimed, taking a deep breath,

her brown eyes sparkling with delight. 'Thank you, James!' She ran to her room, her hands trembling as she fumbled in her eagerness to get ready. He had forgiven her, and she'd thought him hard. If she hadn't run for her room she would have thrown her arms around him and hugged him madly. She smiled. If this was love then she wanted it to go on and on and on. She felt as strong as the mountains, as wide as the world, as high as the sky, and she was glad that love had come to her late like a great burgeoning explosion of exaltation, enveloping, expanding, and transforming her in one breathless moment. Not for her the delicate tiny bud slowly developing, shyly encouraged into life, fearful, fanciful and capricious. She didn't want that ... she wanted just what she had. Oh, she loved James without sham or shame, and she revelled in the knowledge, even knowing that there was no hope of that love ever being returned, nor the physical desire and need for him ever being satisfied.

James talked to Marigold walking across the paddocks, while Joshua stared out of the backpack with wonder in his round eyes, peering down at the dogs, chuckling with joy at the cattle, secure and safe on James' back. It was all new to him, because he had been too miserable to notice anything yesterday. And Shannon walked carefully behind them all, loving each one in turn with her eyes—James tall, lean and tanned, Marigold elfin and leggy and enthusiastic, and Joshua peeping one-eyed from behind his hood.

'There's a pukeko, Shannon.'

She watched the awkward colourful bird scuttle away, flirting its white tail, signalling alarm to all the others. And she glowed because James had spoken to her. Then she saw the Paradise Ducks, flying low to land in the paddock beyond, each matched with its mate as soon as they landed, wandering away in pairs. Lucky ducks, they knew what it was all about.

'Well, there's the fence up, Marigold,' said James. 'Do you think we made a good job of it?'

Marigold tipped her head on one side and gave it a professional scrutiny. 'Perfect.'

'That's right, perfect, but only because you helped. Now we have to get ready for church. What are you going to wear?'

Shannon smiled. James was getting trained to know that what Marigold chose to wear was of vast importance, and it paid to give considerable advance notice if you wanted to hurry.

'Perhaps I should have stayed home and done the washing if we're going to be away all day,' said Shannon as she went under his arm at the gate.

'Did you want to?' he asked with a strange inflection in his voice.

'No,' Shannon replied honestly. 'I wanted to come with you.'

'Good, the washing will keep till tomorrow.' He smiled at her, then turned to close the gate.

Shannon looked down at her feet and saw a dewdrop trapped in the hollow of a clover leaf, a liquid bubble of exquisite perfection and beauty. That was how her love felt inside, a bubble of joy, pure and clean and fresh . . . and James had smiled at her, and he had wanted her to go with him. Would she ever get used to it?

An hour later they walked up the gravel drive to the old church on the rise. If James felt any trepidation at the gossip that would flow because of his three companions, he wasn't showing it. The bells were ringing and he ushered them into a pew near the back just in time for the first hymn. The children were beautifully dressed, and their behaviour matched. Shannon only hoped it would last.

Marigold seemed quite at home singing her heart out, and Joshua, held on James' arm, beamed on anyone who would take notice of him.

Then came the reading, and James put Joshua down on the seat and strode to the front, and as he read in his deep strong voice Shannon knew a swelling of pride that she could hardly contain. She was part of his family just for a time.

'I can't see James,' Marigold protested.

'Shh! Just stand up on the seat and you'll see him. There's no one behind us.' Shannon let go Joshua to help her up, and knew he had crawled out to the aisle. She had moved to get him when she heard Marigold.

In a startled, incredulous and very penetrating voice she demanded, '*Is that God?*'

Crimson, Shannon grabbed her, 'No, it isn't. Shhh!'

'If it's not God, who is it?' Marigold demanded loudly.

'Sit down. Be quiet! It's the Bishop. Haven't you seen one before?' Heads were turned, and shoulders were shaking. James would murder her.

Marigold shook her head. 'No.'

'Well, you can get up again, but you're not to talk.'

'All right.' The awe was still in her eyes.

Shannon turned to gather up Joshua, but to her horror she was too late. Crawling with vigorous speed towards the sound of James' voice, he had reached the chancel steps. Shannon bit her lip. She certainly wasn't going to walk up there with all eyes upon her. James could handle it.

And he did with style. He completed his reading without a flicker of an eye towards where Joshua sat watching him with an adoring smile, then stepped down, catching him in his arms without a break in his stride, and made his way back to Shannon.

'Oh, James, I'm so sorry,' she whispered, then giggled hysterically.

'It's okay,' he whispered back with a grin. 'The man who isn't God is having a bit of trouble keeping a straight face up there.'

Was this James, smiling with her, being understanding? What had happened to Mighty McCabe, who had only contempt for her?

As the service finished, he muttered, 'Get ready to get out . . . fast.'

So that was why they were at the back. Shannon caught Marigold's hand and followed him, close behind the Bishop and Vicar. He was smart. They'd be first out, and away before people could engage them in conversation. But it wouldn't stop them talking.

James was at her elbow. 'We'll take Marigold over to look at the train in the park just for a few minutes. It's a special attraction here in Reefton. Ferrymead, the Historic Museum, wants it, but we've managed to hold on to it so far. Children and visitors love it. It's a Fairlie, one-ended, the only one of its kind in the Southern Hemisphere, perhaps in the world.'

'Watch me!' Marigold was climbing on the engine. Standing up, she stood poised like a bird, then jumped. It must have been at least ten or twelve feet in height. She landed lightly on the green grass, laughing.

'You could have been hurt!' Shannon scolded.

'I wasn't frightened.' Marigold answered scornfully. 'Can I have another go?'

'Not now, we're going to see your mother. Come on.'

The drive was becoming familiar, but it never lost its appeal—the bush-clad hills, the verdant green farms, the wild rivers, and then the sea from

Greymouth to Hokitika. They stopped for a meal,
then drove to the hospital.

A nurse stopped Shannon and the children as they
walked along the corridor. 'Sister would like to see
you before you go in. She'll be in her office.'

'Come in, please. Oh, it's you, Miss Haldane.
Good afternoon, Marigold and Joshua. My, don't
you look flash in your Sunday best! Take a seat,
please. Good, I just wanted to speak to you before
you saw Michelle. We've changed her pills and that
can often be upsetting, but it will only be temporary,
then there'll be a marked improvement. I would
rather you didn't stay long today. She's in bed. Just
go and speak and let her know you're here. I tried
to ring you to stop you driving all this way, but I
couldn't get an answer.'

'We were out on the farm and then at church,'
Shannon told her, her heart sinking. 'Is she worse?'

'No, but she wasn't responding. Don't look so
worried—it's quite a normal procedure. We have to
find the medication that's right for her, then when
she's stabilised she'll shoot away. I think you
shouldn't come again for a week. It's so far, and I
doubt if Michelle will have the energy to talk very
much. The children are thriving, that's the main
thing.'

Marigold had been listening intently. 'God's going
to make her better,' she announced aggressively.

'I'm sure he is, but he has to use us to help her as
well. Now come along with me.'

James looked surprised when they returned so
quickly, but made no comment when Shannon explained the reason. If only she knew what he was
thinking! If only she could share her anxiety with
him—but she couldn't. She might love him, but she
still could not trust him, not about Michelle.

The trip home was quiet. All Shannon's bubbling

new happiness had disappeared. Michelle had tried to be cheerful for the children, but the effort had cost her a lot. Shannon had decided not to mention Mrs McCabe; that could wait till next week. When they arrived home James changed into casual clothes and amused the children while Shannon wrote letters, to William and the girls, and to Simon. Only to William and Simon did she tell the whole story— well, not about the McCabes, but about Michelle and the children, asking Simon about the legal aspects. To the others she wrote a humorous letter about the farm and the animals. It was peculiar the way she missed them all. She had not appreciated the bond that had grown up between them through the years. They were her only family and suddenly they seemed important and very dear. She had thought of them as a burden, a nice burden, but had longed for the day when she could get on with living her own life. Now she found that she couldn't slough off those years like an old skin, and she didn't want to. She wanted to keep her ties with them, to know the happenings in their lives, and for them to share hers. Families were important. Michelle had taught her that.

After dinner when the children were in bed, she and James sat watching T.V. It started to rain heavily, and the wind lashed against the house.

'Blast the weather! The shearers are coming on Wednesday—I hope it picks up. Are you up to feeding half a dozen extra for lunch?'

'Yes. You'll have to tell me what they need.'

'I'll do that. They'll need smokos too—scones and sandwiches, and cakes, at ten and again at three. We'll work it out.'

Shannon liked that. We'll work it out. Together. James hadn't spoken much to her today, but she was grateful that he was talking at all. Even though the programme was interesting, she felt sleepy. Too much drama in her life—she wasn't used to it.

'I'll make supper tonight.' James stretched his long frame in his chair before getting to his feet. Then he suddenly started to laugh. 'Marigold was a classic in church this morning! I could see the congregation's faces, they just gasped, then crumpled. I'll never forget it.'

Shannon exploded again at the memory, and spluttered, 'Then I let Joshua get away. I nearly died, but I couldn't walk up there, not if you paid me.'

'Our first visit to church was a rather shattering experience—give them something to enjoy for weeks.'

He came back with coffee and biscuits. 'I'm worn out. Those kids are mighty exhausting. No wonder Michelle cracked up! You'd have to be in peak physical condition to cope with them day and night single-handed.'

'I'm tired too,' Shannon confessed. 'Perhaps there's an extra strain looking after other people's children, a greater responsibility. When Michelle recovers I think I'll ask them if I can have a couple of weeks there to recuperate. I was so scared of that place, yet each time I visit I'm more aware of the loving attention she's getting. The staff are fantastic.'

'The view alone would be half the cure,' James remarked, then sat silent for a while.

Shannon tried to control her elation. That was the very first time James had spoken naturally about Michelle. She could have mentioned that, far from being in normal health, Michelle hadn't recovered from Joshua's birth when she had to face the loss of Mark, but it was better not to add anything. He wasn't stupid, whatever else he was.

'Shannon, you said you had my mother's address,'

he said suddenly. 'Could you give it to me?'

She got up and went through to her room and came back with the card. She cursed herself for the suspicion in her mind, but felt bound to ask, 'You'll give it back?'

The friendliness disappeared from his face in an instant, and the flint in his eyes was matched by his voice. 'I'll return it. Your lack of trust in me is patently clear,' he added dryly. 'In your opinion, quite obviously, Attila the Hun would have been considered a social benefactor compared to me.'

'How perceptive of you,' Shannon said sweetly. 'Goodnight.' She went to check on the children, then directly to her own room, not even glancing in his direction. He was impossible! How could she trust him with anything that concerned Michelle? She *had* to be wary and watchful. Why, his new softer approach to her could be just a new and devious scheme to win her confidence. She had felt such compassion and sympathy for him last night, such gratitude towards him this morning, and yet she had to double her guard. Loving him had made her much more vulnerable. She longed to believe in him, to admire and respect him, to see only the good in him, but she was the only obstacle standing between him and the children. She was sorry she had made him angry, but she could not afford to let him outmanoeuvre her.

The storm grew worse, the lightning zigzagged from sky to earth and the thunder cracked, then rolled with such violence that it shook the foundations of the house. Shannon could not sleep, so she lay watching the spectacular display. Then she heard Marigold crying, and went quickly through to her, scooping her up in her arms.

'What's the matter, love?' she whispered.

'I'm scared. I *hate* that noise.'

Shannon soothed her and carried her out to the kitchen.

James had come quietly up beside them. 'I know the feeling, Marigold, but you're quite safe. It'll go away in a few minutes. We've had the worst of it.'

Lightning struck close to the house and all the lights went out, then the thunder-clap deafened them.

'Here's a torch, Shannon. Are you frightened?' He put his arm round her.

'Not of the storm,' she said succinctly, 'I'll take Marigold into my bed, we'll comfort each other.'

She heard him laugh as she cuddled down beside the frightened little girl. Wretched man! Had he guessed at the weakness that had come over her when he held her close? Had she been a little slow to move away? What a fool she was, fighting and resisting the very thing she longed to do. It would have been so easy to pretend to be scared of the storm, to move closer to him, to be held close in the dark, feeling the strength and warmth of his body against hers. But then he would have learned of the hunger within her, and he had had enough advantages already. Her emotions were travelling along on a huge and terrifying switchback railway, rushing up over high mountains, then back down into valleys, and around corners and she could not see the finish, joy when he liked her, despair when he was angry, joy when she loved him, despair when she thought of Michelle . . . where would it end?

At last she slept.

She woke to a world fresh washed with rain, sparkling clean in bright sunshine, with wisps of mist clinging to the bush on the hills.

The week rushed by, and she knew she would treasure it, keep it and hold it for years and years. James had changed towards her, a subtle change that defied her to describe, but it was there. The sarcasm was gone, the contempt too. It was as if he had re-structured his thinking about her and was working to establish a good relationship between them. Of course he was still reserved, his motives hidden behind a careful screen of polite consideration for her and the children, but he laughed more often and that was good. She suspected that he changed be-cause of the shearers coming. He would hardly want the district to know that they lived in a state near hostility most of the time. What had brought about the change was less important than the change itself.

He seemed to want the children with him all the time. Each morning he arranged his work so that they could all go with him to move the calves, then he would take them to where he was working with the sheep or cattle in the Land Rover. He took them fencing with him, mending gates, drafting sheep, only leaving them at home when Joshua had to sleep. She would rush through the housework like a whirl-wind, just to be free to go with him.

And each day her love grew, and developed and spread, like a wild luxuriant tropical plant, nour-ished and fed by being constantly in his company. Strongly aware that her very senses and strength deserted her when he came too close, she used the children as a barrier, but when they did accidentally touch, she felt boneless and throbbing with a poignant desire that grew worse instead of better.

On Tuesday she rang the hospital, they suggested that she bring some clothes for Michelle on Sunday.

She flew back to the kitchen, her eyes shining. 'She must be better, James. Oh, I'm so thankful! How about that, Marigold? Mummy wants clothes to wear, she must be able to get up and dress. Isn't that wonderful?'

'Yes. But she hasn't any clothes now.' She turned

to James. 'Will you buy Mummy things like you did for us?'

'I will. I'll go and write a cheque now. We'll go straight into town and post it. She should get it to-morrow. One of the shops will send her up some gear to choose from.'

He went to his desk, and Shannon felt such a wave of love for him that it almost became unbearable. He was always so positive with every decision he made, and so generous. It must have cost him plenty to outfit the children with all new clothes and toys, and he was generous with his time too, and that was even more important.

'Come on, hop in the car, we'll go now. You'll need fresh bread and milk with the shearers coming tomorrow.' He grabbed Joshua up and looked at him. 'No need to change him, just give his face a lick with the cloth.'

Sharron obeyed him, protesting as she followed him out to the car, 'I look a real scruff!'

James eyed her trim figure, dressed in jersey and jeans. 'You look all right to me.'

She sat in the car with a grin a mile wide. If she looked all right to him, there was no more effort needed. She had reached the summit.

As they stood on the street outside the dairy, James suddenly waved to someone along the street. 'There's Mark—I want to see him. Hey, Mark! Come here!'

The effect on Marigold was electric. She turned to where James was waving and flew on tiptoe, her small face lit with joy, towards the tall dark-haired young man coming towards them. Then her face fell and she turned, rushing sobbing at James, kicking him, pummelling him with her small clenched fists.

'You telled a lie, you telled a lie! It's not Mark, *it's not my Mark!*'

'Behave yourself, Marigold! Stop acting like a

crazy child!' He tried to pick her up, but she fought with him, all arms and legs kicking and whirling.

'She thought it was her father, James,' Shannon shouted at him, through a thick voice.

'Oh, dear God,' James muttered. 'Talk to Mark, I'll deal with this.' He grabbed Marigold, still squirming, under his arm and disappeared down a side street.

If he smacks her, I'll kill him! Shannon thought savagely, tempted to follow them and make sure, but the young man was standing in front of her with an amazed look in his eyes. 'What happened there? First time I've ever seen James lose his cool.'

'Your name is Mark. Marigold's father was Mark McCabe, and when James called you she must have thought . . . I don't know what she thought. He died, her father, about six months ago.'

'Yes, I heard about that. Poor kid! I knew Mark well, we grew up together. Look, I'm sorry about this. I wouldn't have it happen for the world.' He was really upset. 'Tell James I'm in a hurry, I'll give him a ring.'

He stood confused for a moment, then thrust his hand in his pocket and came out with some money. 'Look, would you go into that shop and buy her the biggest box of chocolates you can find. Tell her it's from Mark Two—that's what people used to call me when I got around with her father. Tell her I'll come and see her one day. I feel dead rotten about this.' He went off in a hurry.

By the time Shannon had bought the chocolates Joshua was getting very heavy and it was a relief to see James and Marigold coming hand in hand along the street. Marigold's face was still streaked with tears, but she was clinging hard to James, so all must be well.

'Marigold wants new curtains for her room. She

says hers are all faded. I'm shocked that you didn't
tell me how bad they were, Shannon.'

'I'm sorry,' Shannon offered. Obviously he had
been pushed to enormous lengths to win Marigold's
acceptance again. 'What sort of curtains, Marigold?'

'Blues ones with little girls on them.'

'We'll go right in and buy them now. Can you
make them up, Shannon?'

'Sure can,' she said happily, and handed Joshua
over. Trust Marigold to have the colour scheme all
in her mind! She must have lain in bed thinking
about it, and when she was hunting for an excuse for
her tears, it had popped into her mind.

They bought Holly Hobby curtains and a matching bedspread, and the children were delighted, but
James still looked fairly shaken as he drove home.

The next three days were busy with the shearers
in, and Shannon enjoyed the jokes and the laughter,
not to mention the sly innuendoes of the shearing
contractor. She giggled at James' face more than the
remarks—very disapproving. Whether for her reputation or his she would have liked to enquire.

On Sunday they returned to Hokitika, and
Michelle was sitting outside enjoying the sunshine,
dressed in her faded slacks and top. Her large grave
extraordinary blue eyes lit with pleasure as Shannon
and the children came through the lounge and across
the lawn to her.

'You look lovely—oh, Michelle, you look so well!'
Shannon was overjoyed. She had not expected such
a dramatic recovery.

'It's great to see you . . . and the children. What
lovely clothes! James must have spent a fortune on
them.'

Michelle sat with Marigold nestled up beside her
and Joshua on her knee, and they all talked and
talked. The more Shannon described their life on

the farm, the more wonderful James seemed to
Michelle. It wasn't quite the reaction she wanted,
but as far as the children's treatment had gone James
had been without fault. She wanted to reassure
Michelle, but she didn't want her only seeing his
good side. He had an ulterior motive, and she'd
better be aware of it.

'It won't be long before you're home at this rate,'
Shannon suggested when they had exhausted themselves.

'At least another week or ten days,' said Michelle
with a rueful smile. 'You're only seeing me sitting
down. I'm as weak as a kitten, but thank the Lord,
my head is completely clear. I feel terrific.'

'Shouldn't I take Joshua from you? He might be
too heavy for you.'

'No. I love the feel of him back in my arms. I
really have missed them so much, and you must be a
very special person to have cared so well for them,
to have laid aside your own plans to take on the
children and me. I keep thinking about it. . . .'

'Look, you're tired now. We'll have plenty of time
to talk when you get home.' Shannon didn't want to
be thanked. She felt part of this family. 'Oh, did you
get the cheque James posted?' she added.

'Yes, it was far too generous of him. Is he with
you today? I would like to give it back to him. My
own money is supposed to be coming through soon.
I can manage. Would you ask him to come and
speak to me, please? Just for a couple of minutes so I
can thank him.'

'Okay, but you watch James McCabe. He's been
good, I'll admit that, but he is after your children,'
Shannon warned. 'Don't you forget it.'

Michelle looked shocked. 'He's been quite fabulous. How can you say things against him?'

'No trouble at all,' said Shannon, and kissed her

goodbye. 'James will get the kids. I see Joshua's gone to sleep.'

She went out to the car. 'Michelle wants to see you. I left the kids with her. Just for a couple of minutes, she said. She hasn't yet cashed your cheque. She wants to give it back to you.'

'Does she indeed?' His face had that closed look. 'That's ridiculous! She's got nothing of her own.'

He got out of the car impatiently.

Shannon was worried. 'You can go round the end of this building—she's on the lawn there. James, *please* don't upset her. She's just getting better.'

James swung on his heel and glared at her. 'Your opinion of me never changes, does it? What do you think I am? A *monster*?'

'Close,' Shannon said smartly, then spoiled it by giggling as he walked away.

He was gone for ages and, becoming anxious, Shannon crept up to the corner of the building and peeped around the corner. They were chatting away like old friends. She sighed with relief and went back to the car. She shouldn't have worried, Michelle was so beautiful, so soft and vulnerable, she would charm even Mighty McCabe out of his tree.

James was very thoughtful when he came back to the car, except for saying that they were coming down next Wednesday to take Michelle shopping, he hardly spoke a word for the whole trip. As they topped the Reefton Saddle, the whole valley was whited out in fog. Shannon was enchanted. 'Unless you knew that dear little town was there by the river, you wouldn't believe it!' she exclaimed.

'You won't be so pleased with it when you've survived a week of it. Sometimes it lies like that for up to a month in the winter. Good for the stock, as it keeps the frost away, but hard on people.'

'Does the frost hurt the cattle?' Shannon enquired.

'No, stupid. The frost hurts the grass, it shrivels up.'

'You're all charm today,' Shannon observed nastily.

'Sorry, I feel lousy. I've got a splitting headache, and a high temperature. Don't know what it is. I never get sick . . . can't afford to.'

Shannon looked at him anxiously. 'I hope you haven't got that horrible twenty-four-hour 'flu. The shearers were talking about it. They said it's vicious. You ought to stop and see Brad, he'll give you some pills.'

'You talk too much. *I am not sick!*' he snapped, then as if in apology, 'Michelle is really a charming girl. I was surprised.'

'Because she was charming, or because you were wrong about her?'

'One of your most endearing qualities is your total honesty, coupled with an incredible lack of trust and lack of perception.'

'Huh! Michelle has enough trust for both of us. One of us has to keep a watching brief.'

By the time James had the fire lit, Shannon could see that he was very ill. He shouldn't have kept driving, but they said 'flu came on very suddenly, was sharp and violent, then disappeared next day, except for a few which developed a secondary phase.

'Could I get you anything special for dinner?' she offered in a more sympathetic tone.

'No, I don't want a thing. Can you manage the children if I go straight to bed? I'll take a whisky. That might knock it back.'

'Sure, go right ahead. The children will be going early to bed tonight anyway after the trip.'

Cheerfully Shannon cooked a simple meal, bathed the children, then put them down. She had to sit and read to Marigold for a while, because she was over-excited at the thought of her mother coming home, but at last she became drowsy.

Shannon settled down for a quiet night knitting and watching T.V. She had so much to think about. James had liked Michelle, and the other night he had understood her illness. There was every prospect of his accepting them all under his protection, and then . . . and then . . . she would go on her way, not exactly rejoicing, rather with a Mission Accomplished feeling. She wouldn't think of that tonight. Tonight she only wanted to be happy.

Then the telephone rang and it was Simon. Her very first call. They always wanted James. Well, she wanted James always, so it was quite understandable.

'Simon!' How lovely to hear your voice.'

'Hi there. Thought I'd speak to you personally. Your letter sounded somewhat incoherent. You have got yourself involved, haven't you?'

'Yes,' Shannon answered meekly. 'Are you going to say I told you so?'

'I am. You've acted in a totally irresponsible manner. You should have gone directly to the police station in Picton, then they could have taken care of the girl, and returned the children to the proper authorities.'

'You're sounding like a lawyer,' Shannon accused him.

'I am a lawyer! You virtually kidnapped those children. If James McCabe had wanted to force the issue you could have been put on a charge. I've checked it out and he's been granted legal custody by the courts. The children are supposed to be in his care.'

'They are . . . almost,' Shannon protested.

'I have no idea why he allowed you so much say,' Simon went on. 'I'm a bit suspicious of him.'

'So am I,' Shannon remarked agreeably.

'For an entirely different reason. You haven't fallen for him, have you?'

'You're joking,' she said dryly. She would love to see his face if she had told the truth.

'Do you want me to come down? I could hire a plane. . . .'

'No . . . no,' she answered hurriedly. 'It's almost all over now. We went to Hokitika today, and Michelle will be home in a week or so, and I'll be on my way. James liked her, so it will all end quite satisfactorily . . . for them.'

'I could still come. I haven't been on the Coast for years, and I'm missing you more than I thought I would.'

'How complimentary! But please don't come. I wouldn't have a moment to spend with you in private—the children go everywhere with me.' She waited for his comment. She did *not* want Simon here—too complicated.

'Well, I'll meet you in Christchurch later,' said Simon. 'Remember to keep in touch.'

'Yes, Simon dear.'

'Remember too, those children are McCabes legally. You haven't got a leg to stand on. It was just a nicety, a mere formality, to have the mother's approval.'

'Yes, Simon dear. Goodnight, Simon dear, thanks for ringing.'

She hung up and went back to the fire. What was James McCabe up to . . .? It was mind-boggling. He was playing some deep game, and it needed thinking about. Simon *must* be wrong. Perhaps if James simply took Joshua and Marigold, then Michelle might be entitled to have access, and if he wanted her right out of their lives, he had to get her word on it. That must be it, otherwise he would have just taken the children from her at the motel, and she wouldn't have been able to do anything about it. Then again they had arrived unexpectedly, and it would have taken time for him to interview and choose the man he was going to hire to look after them. So he had just accepted her offer for convenience's sake, until he could choose someone more to his liking.

She wished Simon had not rung, she'd been so happy, but now she was back on the treadmill, trying to fathom the depths of James' complicated and devious mind, and she knew how inadequate she was for the job. Michelle would be no help until she finally accepted what he was about, and then it would be too late. Michelle was too trusting, naïvely believing the very best of everyone. The trouble was, if she came here and saw how wonderfully happy the children were, how good James was with them, and the advantages they would have living here and growing up here, she might just give in to him. She was so unassuming, lacking in confidence in herself, that she might sacrifice her own desire to have the children, and for their better good bow out, not realising that she *was* their greatest asset.

Thoroughly upset, she went to bed. She had known it would not be easy when she started pitting herself against McCabe, but she didn't realise just how hard it would be. She was not only fighting him, she maybe wouldn't even have Michelle and the children understanding what she was working at. But she would fight him to the last. Whatever happened she intended to gain legal access for Michelle to come and see the children, and to have them for holidays occasionally. And then she was fighting herself, wanting to give in, wanting to love him freely without all these complexities. Oh, James, she thought, why can't you just admit you're wrong, and say outright that they belong together? She didn't think she could love him more than she did at this minute, but if he did that she'd make an effort, and see if she could find some tiny part of herself that didn't love him totally and bring it into line.

She woke up during the night hearing a strange noise, and was on her feet pulling on her robe before she was fully awake. Which child was it this time? Switching on the kitchen light, she hurriedly peered into the cot, Joshua was sleeping like a tiny angel. Then she tiptoed over to Marigold, and she was scrunched up almost completely under the quilt and her breathing was beautifully slow and even. Puzzled, Shannon went back to the kitchen.

Something had woken her. Could it have been the wekas screeching? She didn't think so, because she was used to them now. Perhaps it had been cats fighting. She stood quietly, listening intently. There it was, someone was groaning and crying out in pain. *James*. It was James having a nightmare. Should she go in? Undecided, she hovered outside his door, moving from one foot to the other. She was often in his room, making his bed, vacuuming and dusting the room, putting away his washed and ironed clothes, but never when he was in it. She was being stupid and prudish, but still she hesitated.

There was another groan followed by a series of mutterings and then a heavy thud. She walked in and flicked the light on.

'What's the matter, James?' Then she stared at the mess. The blankets were off the bed one side and he was on the floor on the other. She hurried round to him. 'Are you ill?'

He was waving his arms about and talking some nonsense about a tractor, then a football match, all jumbled up, and he was shaking with cold, yet the perspiration was pouring off him. He didn't know her, didn't even know she was there.

Shannon went to make the bed, and found the sheets wringing wet. He must have a raging fever. Quickly she made the bed with new linen, then sponged him off with a wet cold cloth and patted him dry, before she half lifted, half dragged him back into bed . . . well, she tried, but he was so big. If he hadn't suddenly come round and recognised her and helped her she would have had to leave him on the floor.

'Whadayadoing, Shannon?' His voice was blurred.

'Sit up, James. Please sit on the edge of the bed. You're very ill. Can you get your pyjama trousers off and put these on?'

He stared at her with glazed eyes, 'Well, I'm not going to let you.'

'That's what I thought. Here you are.' He looked like drifting off again, so she took the wet cloth and wiped his face.

He swore at her, but started to pull his pyjama trousers off, and she left him. She filled two hot water bags, but by the time she got back he had collapsed across the bed. She carefully rolled him one way and freed the blankets, then pulled him back again, putting a hottie at his feet, and another at his back before tucking him in. He was shaking as if with plague, talking and raving nonsense—quite delirious, with his temperature sky-high. That shearing guy had said that that was part of the 'flu. Shannon wished she had come in to see him before she had gone to bed. She went out to get a glass of water in case he needed a drink. There was not much she could do really. It would wear off eventually.

She was only away a few minutes, but by the time she returned James had thrown out the hot water bottles and flung off his blankets. It was going to be a full-time job keeping him covered.

Near morning she was almost exhausted. Half the time he was shuddering with cold and clutching the blankets, the next minute flinging them off with wild thrashing and mutterings. Sometimes he knew her, sometimes he didn't. Surely it would burn itself out soon? But he seemed to get worse. Shannon managed to get him to swallow Disprins dissolved in water and waited hopefully, sitting on the edge of the bed. She only had the light from the hall to work by, because James had swiped the bed light off twice because it was hurting his eyes.

He went quiet for about five minutes and she sighed with relief. Maybe she could leave him and grab a little sleep for herself. She moved the sheet away from his face to see if he had fallen asleep, when he suddenly opened his eyes, sat up and said clearly, 'Sandra! I knew one day you'd come back.'

Before she could move his arms went round her and he pulled her down beside him, his mouth seeking and finding hers, his hands moving over her body. She felt herself drowning in the sweetness of his embrace, hating herself for responding to his demanding mouth but unable to resist. She knew he didn't know who she was, but it didn't matter now. She loved him and wanted him so desperately, and even if she had struggled, she could never have escaped from his arms.

She tried to block her ears to the endearments he was pouring out to her. They weren't for her, they were for Sandra. Gently and tenderly his hands moved over her body, his lips brushing her hair, her ears, her eyes, her throat, then back to her mouth. Her own arms went round him, holding him as she had always longed to, her hands caressing his thick hair, moving down over his strong tanned shoulders and back, knowing there was no turning back now, her own passion mounting on a roaring floodtide to meet his.

Then suddenly he thrust her from him, pushing her violently away, swearing at her, cursing at her, demanding that she leave him alone. With another push he sent her toppling from his bed on to the floor, and she lay there dazed and shaken. She pressed her body against the carpet, hearing him rave above her, waiting for the throbbing in her own body to slacken, knowing that if that bitterness she could hear in his voice changed to appeal and love she would move back, not having the power to resist.

Long minutes passed, and the chill of the early morning made her shiver. Slowly and unsteadily she got to her feet and warily approached the bed. James was sleeping, just like Joshua, just like a baby. Her heart melted with tenderness. Carefully she pulled the bedding over him, putting her hand on his forehead, and found it cool to her touch. She left the room. He was over the worst of it, but something told her she would never be cured of her fever.

The rising sun was pinking the sky as she came back to the kitchen, the bird in the tree was trilling its song. No use going back to bed, she could not sleep now. Quickly she showered and dressed, then lit the potbellied stove, and put the kettle on. She had a little time to sort herself out before the children woke, time to get off the crazy switchback of emotions. Disappointment of unsatisfied desire, exaltation of the love she felt for him.

What kind of fool was she? Laughter bubbled up inside her, welled over and exploded almost hysterically. Happiness, like a bright shining morning light, shafted through her. James had thrown her out, because he had thought she was Sandra. What had she to worry about? What more did she want as proof that Sandra's spell was broken? Appalling though his language had been, she delighted in every vile word he had spoken. He was cured of more than the 'flu. She knew that in his spirit, he was cleansed, purged and whole from five years' captivity. He was free, completely healed. Nothing could survive the furnace that burned with molten fury the bitterness and the guilt, and the pain, and the humiliation that he had stored all these years within his very soul. It had been a purifying experience, consuming the dross of revulsion and anguish, and leaving him drained and so at peace that he had fallen asleep.

She knew now what he had been hiding behind that wall of indifference and hardness and cynicism. Sandra's unfaithfulness must have seared and scarred him so deeply that all the tenderness, and sensitivity in his nature had been blotted out, and he had only survived by building an impregnable wall of pride and arrogance, to hide from everyone his hurt and loneliness. She didn't blame him. She could only admire his courage, and love him all the more. Something had melted in him the day he held Joshua in his arms, and the pain and longing she had seen there must have been the first real warmth he had allowed to reach him for years.

She had thought he was cunningly using his charm and power, to win and dominate the children, and all the time it was he who had been warmed and reborn under the influence of the beautiful boundless, uncomplicated love they gave out so freely. The children adored him and showed him that without subterfuge or adult caution, and he had softened as a direct result of that love. Shannon had spent endless hours trying to get behind his mind, and now she had it handed over on a plate, and she didn't want to know. How could she dare now try and take those children from him? Oh, it was too complicated and deep for her. It was a relief to have Marigold come pattering out to warm herself at the stove.

'James has been very ill, Marigold. We'll have to do all the work on our own today. Do you think we can?'

'Course we can,' Marigold said scornfully. Then her eyes shone. 'You mean moving the calves . . . all by ourselves?'

'Just that,' Shannon replied with a grin. 'Let's get Joshua up, I think James will sleep all day.'

It was exciting getting the baby in the pack and loosing the dogs. The dogs went hysterical with joy, rolling in the frost, jumping up on her with happy barks, almost bowling her over. She felt fairly confident that she could manage. After all, they had watched James each day, and were fairly skilful at helping him run out the thin plastic-coated string, and hook it on the light standards. She carefully took out the fuse by the gate, and let the calves run through into the fresh grass. It was a breeze.

'How about that, Marigold?' she smiled. 'Did we do a good job?'

'Perfect,' came the expected response. 'Can we move the sheep now?'

'No, we'll go home now and see how James is. This is the only job that has to be done each day.'

She replaced the fuse, feeling a certain exhilaration, knowing James would be really pleased with their efforts. How she loved this valley, ringed with bush-clad hills, and backdropepd by the snow-clad mighty Alps. She didn't ever want to leave, not the farm, not the children, and most of all, *not James*. It couldn't happen, that she would have a place here, but it was nice to dream about, as she walked home. But reality was that soon she would be free to go, free to wander the world, to run before the wind, and there was no joy in the thought.

CHAPTER EIGHT

JAMES slept all day Monday. Shannon took him cups of tea, and told him about moving the calves. He had been grateful, but fell asleep even while she stood there.

It suited her very well. She needed a day to herself before she had to face him at close quarters. What if he remembered her being in his bed? Worse than that, her response to his lovemaking? She busied herself sewing Marigold's new curtains on an old style sewing machine she'd found in a cupboard. Once oiled and cleaned it flew over the material. If James liked her efforts she would put new curtains up everywhere—not that she didn't love the house just as it was.

The next morning they walked around the farm, and she watched James carefully, from a safe distance. He had a quiet thoughtfulness about him, his mind obviously not on farm work, but he *had* been very ill. Several times he sat down and rested, his eyes on the horizon but not seeing it. Very like William when he was playing chess games in his mind.

Shannon also was busy thinking. Just because she now understood him better, that did not mean she had to abandon all caution. She knew his need of the children, but she also knew Michelle's need. She believed Michelle would slide back into depression if she lost the children. James was tough, he had proved that, he would recover. She sighed. Really nothing had changed. She was a rock sheltering Michelle and the children from James' determined purpose and plan. Sometimes she felt more like a small pebble in his path rather than a rock, but she might slow him up a little. She would give it her best shot; the trouble was that she was pulled in several directions at once.

He was planning something, she was sure of that. He was hardly even aware of her and the children.

From the moment she got up on Wednesday she sensed something different about James. There was new energy in his step, a sense of urgency in his actions, and a rare impatience with the children.

'No, Marigold, you aren't coming with me this morning. You stay and help Shannon. Remember we're going down to see your mother today.'

'We don't slow you up all that much,' Shannon protested, as much disappointed as Marigold. Well, more, because she loved the morning walk with James and the children.

'Don't argue!' he snapped. 'I've said you're not going. The fog is down and it's too cold for the children. You'll be busy enough getting the washing done, and dressing them ready for town. I want to be away at nine. I promised Michelle we'd be there at eleven, and the drive won't be easy as there's a lot of ice about.'

'I want to go with *you*, James,' Marigold wailed forlornly, and tried to get past him to her coat and gumboots.

He grabbed her up and deposited her on a chair by the stove, 'You're much cosier here. Do what I tell you—sit still. You can help Mummy choose her new clothes when we get to Hokitika. That will be fun.'

'No, it won't. I *want* to go *with* you!' Marigold burst into a flood of tears.

'Well, you can't.' James strode out the door, slamming it behind him.

Joshua had been waiting patiently to be picked up, and when he realised he had also been abandoned he roared with rage.

It took her ages to coax them into a happier frame of mind, and Shannon was very thoughtful as she cleared the breakfast table. There was something new going on that she did not understand. James was terribly eager to get to Michelle. She had been so pleased to see his change in attitude on Sunday, being thrilled that they had reached some sort of understanding. It had excited her, loving Michelle as she did, and being thrilled also at the tremendous improvement in her health and outlook. She had been so certain that when Michelle recovered James would know he had been wrong in his assessment of her character, and it looked as if she was being proved right. He had been really charming to Michelle. Then why this sense of foreboding ... almost fear? Was all this charm a new scheme of James' to get Michelle's confidence, so that she would agree that the children were better off with him? Was this fresh evidence of his generosity in buying her new clothes, and actually taking a day off work to chauffeur her round the shops to choose her wardrobe hiding a deeper, darker motive? Was he putting Michelle under such a sense of obligation that she would agree to almost anything he suggested? Was he trying to buy her off? Did he see victory in the offing?

Marigold stood on a chair at the sink helping Shannon do the dishes, while Joshua disembowelled the pot cupboard. Shannon dashed in and out from the washhouse, swiftly changing the loads of washing, and popping them into the dryer. There would be no drying outside today because the whole world was wrapped in cottonwool fog. She could hardly even see the orchard trees or the firs. She hurried to empty the ashes from the stove.

It was a race against time. She made the beds, contented herself with merely vacuuming the kitchen and lounge, then tidied away the pots and pans and dressed the children. Oh, she still had to dress herself. Her tan trouser suit would be warm and practical for travelling with the children. As she zipped up her slacks she heard James call.

'You ready yet? I'll just have a quick shower, be with you in two ticks. You'd better look after Joshua, he's tipped the ashes over.'

Shannon ran to the porch and there was Joshua crowing with delight as he flung handful after handful of ashes in different directions. He was covered in them. She could have wept.

'How did he get out here, Marigold?' she asked as she stripped off his cute blue overalls and stood him on the sink to clean him.

'When James opened the door,' Marigold informed her. 'I told him not to.'

This was going to be a great day, Shannon thought grimly, as she pulled a clean jersey and overalls on Joshua. Damn McCabe! She had to do all this extra and he was blocking the bathroom as well. She brushed Joshua's silky hair and dropped a kiss on his small glowing face.

'There you are handsome, keep clean. Let me look at you, Marigold. Ah, you're beautiful. Give me a kiss. Keep an eye on your baby brother while I sweep up the porch, and have a wash.'

'I will, Shannon,' Marigold said importantly.

'You ready?' James came out carrying Joshua. 'Really, Shannon, there's no need for you to be doing extra housework this morning. I told you we'd be leaving at nine. Come along, Marigold, you know how to be on time, which is rare in a female.'

Shannon stood up with the shovel and brush in

her hand, and cast a withering look at James, immaculately dressed in a well-cut tweed jacket, knit shirt, and dark slacks. She felt like flattening him. There was no melting in her heart as she glared at his handsome superior face.

'You can wait while I wash my face and hands . . . and I have to fill Joshua's bottle.'

'You should have had all that done. You've had plenty of time. I'll put the kids in the car.'

In wordless rage, Shannon raced for the bathroom, washed sketchily, threw bottle, biscuits, books and nappies into a basket and picked up her handbag.

As she climbed in and slammed the door she said through clenched teeth, 'What did your last slave die of?'

He roared with laughter and started the car, driving carefully out to the main road, then accelerating sharply. He talked and laughed with the children in a rare good mood.

Shannon gradually relaxed, but she still felt untidy, and slightly gritty, inside and out. She hadn't even had time to put on any make-up, or even brush her hair.

It was a fast trip in spite of the patches of frozen ice, and once over the Reefton Saddle they left the fog behind and the sun shone brilliantly. It was a gloriously fine winter day, and her cheerfulness increased. Michelle was well enough to go shopping, she'd soon be home. Life wasn't half bad. Even James looked pleasant in the sunshine.

How funny to be loving him madly, yet fully aware of his every fault. Shannon had always supposed love was blind. But she wasn't blind and she wasn't stupid, and she knew James McCabe was up to something tricky today. She'd watch him like a hawk. Understanding him better did not mean that she would let him have it all his own way.

Michelle was standing by the ramp waiting for them, dressed in her well washed jeans and faded blue jumper. Her soft fair hair shone like molten gold on her shoulders. Her smile was brilliant.

'Michelle had better have the front seat, Shannon. Hop in the back with Marigold,' said James as he braked sharply, and then hurried towards Michelle.

'I was just going to do that,' Shannon muttered after him, and held the door open to greet Michelle. 'You look *terrific*.'

'I'm still a bit wobbly,' Michelle answered. 'But I get there as long as I don't hurry.' She leaned forward to Shannon. 'Friend, I just haven't got the words. . . .' Tears formed in her extraordinary blue eyes.

'There's none needed,' Shannon replied huskily. 'Get in, the children are so excited.'

James closed the door carefully behind Michelle, then went round to the front of the station wagon to the driver's seat, leaving Shannon to join Marigold without any of the same courtesy he had shown Michelle. He really was playing the gallant! But Shannon's heart was singing. Michelle was laughing with the children. Even in one week since they had last seen her, the sharp outline of her face had filled out, giving the contours of her perfect face a new and greater beauty. In spite of her fragility, Shannon thought she was the most beautiful girl she had ever seen.

'Can I sit on your knee, Michelle?' Marigold pleaded, her small face aglow with love.

'No,' James told her sharply. 'Your mother's not strong enough for that yet.'

'Oh, really I am. I've hungered for her. Please, James.'

'Okay, pass her over, Shannon. This is your day,

Michelle, you're the boss. What shop do you want to go to first?'

'Would Addisons be not too much trouble? You could park right by the door. I can't walk very far,' Michelle said apologetically. 'And I'd like to go to the Post Office first to get my money. The Sister arranged for my benefit to be transferred.'

'I gave you a cheque for two hundred dollars.'

'But I can't take your money, when I now have my own. You've given me too much already . . . and the children's gear.'

'You certainly can use my money,' James told her. 'We had that all out on Sunday. You left Shannon in charge of the details, and we made an agreement that I would provide everything you and the kids needed for six weeks. I'll brook no argument. It's my pleasure.'

Shannon sat silent in the back seat. There was something very strange going on. James' tone was warm and real, she could sense his sincerity. Had he had a complete and dramatic change of heart? It would be wonderful if it was true, and if it was false, and he was only acting, then someone should nominate him for an Oscar. She would remain unconvinced till further proof. He could do a proper snow job on Michelle, but she, Shannon, was not so naïve or trusting.

They all went into the store together, and James quickly demanded and got a chair for Michelle to sit on while attendants hovered helpfully near.

'My sister-in-law, Mrs McCabe, has lost all her luggage,' he informed the head of the department. 'You're Mrs Anderson, aren't you? I meet Bruce at all the Federated Farmers meetings.'

'That's right. How nice of you to remember me, Mr McCabe.' The attractive woman was obviously pleased.

'Great. Now we'll start from the skin out. Half a dozen of everything, in the underwear line, stockings, the lot . . . the very best in everything. You understand? Joshua and I will leave you ladies to choose these things. Call me if you have any difficulties.'

He walked off with the baby on his arm, towards the toy department.

'Oh, isn't he kind!' Michelle said somewhat breathlessly. 'I'm just overwhelmed.'

'He is overwhelming,' Shannon admitted a little sourly.

Marigold was in her element, and Shannon felt her doubts slip away when she saw how much joy Michelle and her daughter were getting from the beautiful range of choice. How long it must have been since Michelle would have been able to buy anything for herself, James *was* generous, and he was making this day a day to remember. She felt rather small and mean to be having these niggling fears within.

At last Michelle said with a sigh, 'That's all I need. I feel extravagant—it's more than I'll ever need for years.'

Mrs Anderson waved James across. 'Will this be all now, Mr McCabe?'

'Certainly not! She has to have dresses, skirts, slacks, jerseys—the lot.' He hefted a large suitcase on to the counter. 'When this is full, I'll be satisfied.'

'No, James, I'll not let you,' Michelle protested. 'I *would* like a new pair of jeans and a jersey, but that's all. Even if I wanted to accept, I'd never have the strength to try things on. It's as much as I can do to dress myself in the mornings.'

'Here, Shannon, you take Joshua, he's getting restless,' James ordered. 'I'll deal with Michelle.'

Shannon started out of the store, but James caught her at the door. 'I've been thinking—we'll all need

a meal after this, and a picnic would be better for
the kids. There's a good bakery, round by the clock
tower. Here's money and the car keys. You get a
box of goodies, cakes, sandwiches, cans of drink,
some fruit if you can, and we'll drive out to the Lake.
Michelle would like that.'

Wonderingly Shannon stared after him. James was
a completely different person. He liked Michelle, and
he was getting a great kick out of spending money
on her. He must be trying to make up for all the
hardness his family had shown her. How he must
regret those ugly things he had said about her!
Shannon felt like crying. It was almost too good to
take in.

When she came back, James was standing impatiently on the street. He had the big case in one
hand and Marigold swinging on the other. He
quickly stowed the case in the boot, then went back
into the store.

Marigold and Shannon got in the back seat.

'You should see Mummy, *she's lovely*! James
brought her a beautiful . . . um . . . a beautiful thing.'
Marigold was breathless.

James came out with Michelle on his arm and
Shannon knew what Marigold meant. Michelle was
wearing the most gorgeous mulberry jump suit in
crushed velvet. It had batwing sleeves, and a deep
vee at the neck, and the soft blue scarf at her throat
added the final touch. She looked fabulously elegant.
She was a tall girl, almost up to James' shoulder,
and they made a startlingly handsome couple. She
was holding on to James' arm for support, and he
was laughing at her.

Something cold clutched Shannon's heart. Was
that going to be the solution to his family's problems?
Had James fallen for his brother's widow? Oh, that
was ridiculous. He was a confirmed bachelor—well,

he had been after Sandra. Brad said so.

As the car moved off James announced, 'We're off to Lake Kaniere for a picnic. How do you like that idea, Michelle?'

'I love it. Oh, I've never had a day like this in my whole life!' She turned in her seat to face Shannon. 'You'll love it too. It's always been one of my favourite places. Wait till you see it!'

'You're sure it won't be too much for you, Michelle? We could go to Cass Square or out to the beach?' James asked a trifle anxiously.

'No, of course not. I must be back by two-thirty for my pills, but it won't take us long, will it?'

'Hardly half an hour's drive,' he assured her with a flashing smile. 'But I don't want you to do too much the first day out. There's plenty of time ahead of us.'

Again, the fear pierced Shannon's heart, making it hard to breathe. She looked at him, relaxed and confident and oh, so good-looking. Now she knew how much she loved him. Now she knew it wasn't just a temporary thing, a thing of flesh and desire. It was deep and real, of body, soul and spirit, of life and breath and being. She took a deep breath and held it, then slowly let it go. This pain, this fear that was slicing at her, would ease. It would because it was unbearable, and she could not live with it. She could not examine it, not here with them all watching. Another breath. Good, it was going. She would just pretend it wasn't happening . . . until she got home, until she was alone.

She forced herself to look at the bush-clad hills, the snowy mountain peaks, the ferns and native trees, look anywhere but the front seat, listen to anything but the blending of their voices.

It was pure relief to arrive, to busy herself with feeding the children. She shared a glass of sparkling wine with James and Michelle which he had thoughtfully purchased with glasses at a small township on the way out. She drank to Michelle's happiness, with true thanks for her recovery, blanking out all the implications.

'You're very quiet, Shannon,' James said sharply. 'And you're pale. Are you not well? You haven't eaten anything.'

Shannon forced a laugh. 'First time I've ever heard you complain about me being quiet! Usually you say I talk too much. And I do have a bit of a headache. I'll just pack up the remains of our grand picnic, and take the children for a walk along the shore, while you and Michelle sit in the sun and chat.'

'Oh, but I want to talk to you,' Michelle protested. 'You've cared for my children. You've given me a reason to live. That night I met you, I'd run my course . . . I couldn't face another minute. Now, I want to get to know you. Send James with the children.'

But James did not offer. So Shannon smiled at her, 'We'll have lots of time to talk. I love you too, and your children, but I'd like to try and walk this headache off before we travel home.' She quickly packed the leftovers and James placed the box in the boot.

Michelle said sympathetically, 'Sorry about the headache, I was being very selfish. Could we keep the children here? They're awfully noisy.'

'No. There are swings along there, they'll enjoy a play.' She picked Joshua up and took Marigold's hand, and walked slowly away.

The Lake was incredibly beautiful, a blue jewel set in green beauty, and so still that it captured in reflection the snow-clad grandeur of the Southern Alps and, down to the tiniest detail, the flax bushes, and gaily painted motorboats.

Marigold ran ahead and was swinging vigorously when Shannon reached her. 'Want a push?'

'I can push myself,' she said indignantly. 'I can go higher.'

Shannon sat on the neighbouring swing with Joshua on her knee. 'I can go higher than you!' she challenged.

'I can beat you,' Marigold laughed, her small face lighting up. She stood up on the seat, thrusting her slender body forwards and backwards, swinging higher and higher.

Shannon pretended to be working hard at beating her, but really she was revelling in the fearlessness of Marigold. How could she love this child who wasn't hers so very much? How could she bear to leave them? She held Joshua close till he squirmed in protest. Something was tearing her apart, but she could not even cry. That would have to wait.

Michelle had said something about not having ever to carry more than you could bear. That there was always a way out? Perhaps that was only for those who had the faith of a little child, like Marigold, like Michelle. She felt she was dying inside, internal bleeding as they said after accidents. She *was* being stupid. She had her way out, to travel, to be free, to run before the wind.

The horn sounded, and she saw James and Michelle had driven along the road to pick them up. She had only looked back once, but they had not seen her, gold hair and black together engrossed in each other. She collected the children and joined them.

'Sorry to interrupt,' James offered. 'That looked like fun, but we must have Michelle back on time or they'll never let us borrow her again.'

'I'm going to eat and eat and eat,' said Michelle

with a laugh. 'Then I'll get stronger very fast and be able to run and play with the kids. Oh, how I envied you swinging with them!'

Not as much as she had envied Michelle, Shannon thought bitterly, then hated herself for her unlovely thoughts. It was truly a wonderful solution, a perfect solution. She was an ugly, ugly, selfish person, not to be jubilant for them. She was humiliated to find such selfishness in her character. She was much worse than James had ever been. And he was improving, getting better and better, and she was getting worse. That would teach her to be critical of others.

At the hospital, they were a little early, so they sat talking in the car in the sunshine. Suddenly Shannon could not bear the intimate happiness of them all.

'I'm going to walk down the hill,' she announced. 'I've always wanted to do it, ever since the first trip up here. The view is fantastic. It will give you a bit of time with the children on your own.' She kissed Michelle quickly. 'We'll soon have you home. Keep eating!'

She walked away fast, so they would not see the tears spilling down her cheeks. The sea was sparkling blue, the town below bright colours and through the blur of tears, they were turned into rainbow-fringed fairyland.

She knew that James and Michelle were not even aware of what was happening to them. They were just delighting in each other's company, opening up to each other's personalities. But Shannon knew. She had watched James too closely for weeks not to notice this dramatic change. And they were made for each other. In looks and in every way they would complement each other, James strong and protective and stable and Michelle with the gentle loving nature would soften him the little that was needed. And the children would grow up on the farm, thriving, being extended, developing into wonderful teen-agers and then adults, and she would never see them. Oh, she would promise to come back, but she never would. She couldn't bear that.

By the time she reached the foot of the hill, James drew up beside her and leaned across to open the door. 'Hop in, Shannon. Would you like me to drive back into town and get you some Disprins?'

Shannon shook her head wordlessly.

'My word, Michelle told me off a treat after you left! She's worried that the kids are too much for you. You've had too many broken nights with Joshua, but I think he's okay now that his tooth is through. Tomorrow, I'll take the kids all day, and you can have a complete rest.'

'It won't be necessary. But thanks just the same.'

Marigold was standing behind her and put her thin little arms around Shannon's neck. 'I love you. You're crying, does your head hurt a lot?'

Shannon fished out her handkerchief and dried her eyes. 'Not a bit now, after your cuddle. And I was crying because I'm so pleased that your mummy is all better.'

James was whistling his theme song. 'You'll be my breath when I grow old.' Was he going to trans-fer that to Michelle? Oh, was he one happy guy . . . right on top of the world. Even that thought didn't hurt. It was quite wonderful, this nice little secure cocoon, but she must not tear at it in curiosity. If it holed, she would be at the mercy of that pain again. She could move around in it, try it for size, but be aware of the limits. Outside, like a primitive pre-datory animal, the pain waited to savage her to a bleeding pulp. She could talk and laugh with James and the children, in perfect safety . . . that was enough for now.

She could even think about James and Michelle

living together and that didn't hurt either, which
pleased her. It had been horrible being jealous of
Michelle. If it had been any other girl who had
roused his interest, she would have fought her tooth
and claw, but it was Michelle, and that was different.
Michelle needed love—hers, and the children's and
James', and his mother's love too. Michelle deserved
the very best.

Shannon thought about Michelle coming home,
growing stronger, going out on the farm, and had
nothing but delight in the thought. Then she started
to think of her own future, about leaving the farm,
and she felt the pain pierce her like a knife. She
discarded that thought. It was just to be a day-at-a-
time living. She could handle that. One day at a
time.

Next morning something warned her not to go
out with James and the children, so she made some
flimsy excuse. She experimented all that first day
learning what she could do and think without pain,
exploring the boundaries. She must not get too close
to James, physically. She must not fight with him.
No more needling him, just in case her emotion got
out of control. She didn't feel the loss, really, she
had no desire to scratch the surface and find what
made him tick. She had used it as a method to discover the man underneath the careful mask, and she
had found a real man, someone to respect and
admire, but more than that, someone she knew now
would never hurt Michelle or the children. She loved
the man she had found beneath the arrogant, domineering front, loved him beyond anything she could
ever have imagined.

She laughed as she did the washing . . . his washing. Anyone who could feel romantic about dirty
jeans and socks just because someone they loved had
worn them must be crazy. And it was a delight to

run his bath when she heard the tractor turn in at night, or heard him ride in with his dogs after mustering. Little things for his comfort occupied her day with pleasure. She asked could she buy the new curtaining for the lounge and when he agreed, used that as an excuse not to go out the second day. Not that he took it kindly.

'What's wrong with you, Shannon? You're awfully quiet. It's not natural!'

She smiled sweetly. 'I want the house looking super for when Michelle comes home.'

'But I thought you liked coming out with the kids. We found a wild cat's nest in a hollow log yesterday. The kittens were great. You would have loved them. Down by the Old Mill paddock.'

'The children told me, remember?'

'But wouldn't you like to see them yourself?' His smile was endearing.

The pain gnawed at the edge of her cocoon and she snapped, 'Not really. It was fascinating at first, but it gets a bit . . . *boring*.'

'*Boring!*' He had slammed angrily out of the house, and Shannon had laughed because her security blanket was still working.

When she collected the mail, there were two letters for her. Last week she would have been thrilled, it would have been new evidence of her belonging to the farm. Today she knew it was just a very temporary address. Looking back she realised how blind she had been. That very first day at the motel she had been puzzled at James' sudden volte-face, and had not connected it with his having seen Michelle. That must have been his reason for taking them all on, and providing so wonderfully for them.

She opened the delicately perfumed envelope first, keeping the one with William's familiar handwriting until last. It was from Mrs McCabe . . . a letter of deep thankfulness and gratitude. James had evidently contacted her and straightened things out between them, and she was invited to the farm when Michelle came home. She gave Shannon all the credit for having brought about such a wonderful reconciliation.

It was wonderful news. Shannon was delighted to think of them back together as a family, but she deserved no thanks. She had just bawled James out in a terrible fashion. He had done it all by himself, and his speed amazed her. She could only admire him, and the spirit of forgiveness in him that was helping him rebuild his family. But he could have shared it with her. Had he shared it with Michelle? But Michelle was family.

And her stepfather's letter didn't help much either. 'Glad you've found a man worth loving. I'd like to meet him. Greatly pleased that you've decided to write a script for your own life, instead of the one your father edited . . . you're really finding yourself in the Wild West.' And she had not even said one word about loving James in her letter.

In the evening he returned to the discussion, when the children had gone to bed. She had stopped going into the lounge after dinner, and stayed in the kitchen sewing as if her life depended on it. She had even chosen colours that Michelle would like, blues and golds.

James leaned against the table watching her intently. 'What do you mean, you find farm life boring?'

'Just that I do.' She shrugged her shoulders. 'I'm one of those people who gets a pash on everything new, then I lose my enthusiasm and it becomes dull.'

'I don't believe it,' he said flatly.

'It's immaterial to me whether you believe me or

not.' She stitched carefully along a hem, concentrating on a straight seam.

'Then it's fortunate that Michelle is recovering. If you'd got control over the kids you'd have fooled around for a while till they bored you and then bunged them in a home.'

'More than likely,' she smiled at him wickedly. It was lovely inside her cocoon.

'You stuck to chess all right.' He was looking puzzled and disbelieving. 'You're not giving me a true reason for your behaviour. You're exactly the same as you've always been with the kids and with Michelle. It's me, isn't it? What have I done to hurt you?'

'Not a thing.' She would not meet his eyes.

'There's something. You're up to something. And it started . . . I can almost put a time on it. Sunday night—the night I was sick. What happened?'

She could not help herself. A crimson tide swept over her face and down her body. She bit her lip nervously, then jumped up from the machine. 'If you're to stand over me, cross-questioning me, then I'm going to bed. You've made me sew a crooked seam!'

He stepped forward and put his arms on her shoulders, not biting in the way they had the last time he had wanted to speak to her, but almost lovingly.

'Shannon, Shannon, don't do this to me. We've had our differences, but you've always been honest—painfully honest, if I may say so. Since you've come here, you've made me face issues that have been buried for years. You've made me look at myself, which hasn't been easy. I'm tremendously grateful that you stepped in when you did. You can't suddenly become sulky. . . .'

'I'm not sulky!' Shannon protested, trying to shrug

away from him. When she didn't succeed she burst out, 'I can't bear you to touch me—let me go!'

He stepped back in surprise. 'I've never touched you. Or have I? I can't remember much about Sunday night, except you were there sometimes and then you weren't. I must have been out of my head a lot of the time.'

The phone rang, and Shannon jumped at the excuse to get away, but flinging over her shoulder, 'How would you know? You're like that most of the time.'

Within seconds she was back, 'Brad needs a partner for a game of golf on Saturday afternoon, and he said to ask you, if you're not keeping me in purdah, could I have time off?'

His blue eyes went flinty. 'Suit yourself.'

'Then I'll go. You want to play patriarch, give it a whirl on your own for an afternoon and evening.'

'You're bored with the kids too?' he demanded.

'Am I so transparent?' she taunted him, then returned to the phone.

He stood there watching her as she packed up her sewing. 'I've hurt you, and I do apologise. Will you accept that?'

The pain was back ripping at her. She also wanted to go back to last week when they had enjoyed themselves so much, but it wasn't possible. Something had died in her at the top of the hill at the hospital ... it was called hope. She could fight against a memory, she could fight an empty heart and an empty house, but not against Michelle. That was not possible.

She put the sewing machine away and looked straight at him for the first time since Wednesday, hoping the sadness she felt wasn't naked in her eyes. She spoke softly.

'Yes, I accept your apology, but it's not necessary,

James. You've given me a very happy time here, you've nothing to apologise for. I have. I've been behaving quite badly these last few days, and I hope you'll forgive me. I have problems that you don't know about. Let's leave it at that.'

'I'd like to help, if you'd let me.'

He was so dear, so very dear. 'No, but thanks anyway. Goodnight.'

It came out thickly, and she turned away quickly, heading for her room, not caring if he had seen the tears. She was entitled to weep sometimes.

She cried for a long time, not noisily, but quietly into her pillow. Gradually she stopped weeping and just lay looking out at the stars, seeing their beauty and remoteness, hearing the wekas screeching their mournful call. She seemed to have lost her cocoon of safety, and with dry eyes she grieved for what might have been. She noticed the light still shining out from the lounge windows, which meant James was not sleeping either.

Next morning he waited and had breakfast with them. 'I'd like you to come with us this morning— and before you start inventing excuses, I'll remind you that I pay you, and therefore if you make me I'll assert my authority and order you to come.'

Shannon, her face pale and her eyes enormous, tried to think up some cutting answer, but none came. She was too tired, and she didn't want to hurt him ever again.

'If it's that important, I'll go,' she said quietly.

'It is,' he answered cryptically. He got up from the table. 'I'll do a few bits and pieces, then I'll come back for you all.'

'I'm happy,' Marigold burbled. 'It's not fun without you, Shannon.'

'My sentiments exactly,' said James.

Shannon looked up quickly and caught his blue

eyes on her and turned away. He was looking at her
with compassion, with kindness, with something she
couldn't name, but it sent her pulses racing. He was
so happy the way things were working out he wanted
to be kind to her too, and thought he would achieve
it by dragging her round behind him, and showing
her some new birds, and a few kittens. She wished
the cure was that simple.

She was surprised to find him sitting in the Land
Rover when she had dressed the children.

'We're going up on the Pakihi, when we've fed
the cattle,' he told her.

'You're the boss,' she said as she lifted Marigold
in, and climbed in with Joshua.

'You'd better believe it,' he said with a cheerful
grin, and whistled the dogs as he drove off.

She felt his good mood was weighing on her like a
heavy cloud. She would have to try and match it.
She just needed to get her second wind. Like a long-
distance runner, she seemed to have burned up all
her energy in the first stages of the race, but she'd
come back, because she had to. There were another
two or three weeks to go.

When the fence was moved, James drove back to
the house and across the paddock to the left of it,
stopping to open a big white railway gate, and then
driving over the lines, through another gate, and on
to a gravel road.

As he walked back to close the gates, Shannon felt
cold fingers squeezing her heart. She knew where
they were heading. They were going to the house on
Blue Ridge. He must be going to get her opinion on
it, for furnishing, for curtains . . . preparing it for
Michelle. . . . He could have spared her that. But
then he didn't know what her problem was. She still
had some secrets.

As he drew up in front she looked out across the

farm. From up here high on the plateau she could pick out all the places they'd been on the bottom farm. She could have a bird's eye view of the house, the calves feeding, the Black Pine paddock where they'd spent one wonderful afternoon picking up wood for the open fires. It was a fantastic situation, surrounded by native bush, and she could see for miles. She could even see the white cross on the hill above Reefton. Well, she was between a rock and a hard place now, and where was *her* help?

James had not spoken, but she knew he was looking at her. She hurriedly opened the door and lifted the children out.

'Come on, have a look round and tell me what you think of it. I suppose I should have let it out, but I could never bring myself to do that. I chose the site, I chose the plan, I built it for my wife, and I didn't care to have strangers trampling through it.'

She followed him through it, not speaking, but admiring the clean modern lines, the ranch slider door which gave an uninterrupted view across to the river miles away. It had everything, well designed, architecturally pleasing, and he should be very happy here with Michelle.

He put Joshua down. 'You're big enough to walk, mate. I'm getting tired of carrying you.'

As if understanding, Joshua laboriously got to his feet and stood upright and for the first time, took three steps, beaming with happiness, waiting for his rightful applause.

Shannon grabbed him. 'You're a wonderful boy, so very clever. I love you.' She buried her face in his soft stomach, making him laugh.

'And I love you,' said James from somewhere behind her. 'And I've brought you up here to ask you if you'll marry me, and live in this house with me. I know this isn't the most romantic proposal, but I can't wait any longer.'

Shannon put Joshua down, but instead of turning towards him stared out the window. She doubted her ears were actually transmitting the words correctly.

'I think I fell in love with you the first time I met you. You were so sparky for your size. I'd never met anyone like you. You made me face myself, as I said last night, and it wasn't a pretty sight. Of course I didn't admit it then—I just wanted to flatten you. Then you said you couldn't even bear to breathe the same air as me, and one night when I was playing the piano that song came into my mind, and as I played it I knew I loved you and that you would be my breath when I grew old.'

Shannon turned and flew into his arms. It had been for her all the time. It had been her song. 'Oh, James, I love you so much.'

His arms folded her in. 'I thought you did, then you let something come between us. I wanted to wait for Michelle to come home before I asked you to marry me . . . sort of to preserve the proprieties. But when you switched out the light in yourself, I couldn't see. You are my light, bringing me back from dead years. I'd even forgotten how to laugh.'

'I thought you'd fallen for Michelle, and I couldn't bear it,' Shannon confessed, 'even though I loved her.'

'You'll see plenty of her,' James told her. 'She'll be your neighbour, living in the Homestead. It was to be Mark's, now it will be Joshua's. I wanted her to get well, and I thought if she knew she was welcome to stay at the farm that her recovery would be speedier . . . and I do like her. But I love you, Shannon.' He laughed. 'Promise me you'll wear that sexy nightie on our honeymoon.'

'*Oh, James!*' Then she giggled. 'I'll buy you a matching one!'

'You dare!' He held her closer still and as his lips found hers the switchback gathered speed. She flung her arms about him, not caring where it carried her, only that James loved her.

Harlequin® Plus

A MOST UNUSUAL BIRD

As a New Zealander, Mary Moore is bound to know a lot about kiwis. For the kiwi is New Zealand's national symbol and can be found nowhere else in the world.

Formally called the apteryx, it is a unique little bird commonly known as the kiwi—a word that echoes the shrill mating cry of the male. Not only does the kiwi have an unbirdlike cry, it also has an unbirdlike appearance and behavior: whiskers that resemble those of cats and small stunted feathers that look like hair. It burrows into the earth as if it were a mole and runs rather than flies! The kiwi *does* have wings, but they are short and stumpy protrusions that cannot propel the bird through the air. This inability to fly renders the unfortunate creature a "sitting duck" for predators—including man.

As a result, the almost defenseless kiwi faced extinction not so long ago. Now, however, the birds are protected by law and found mostly in sanctuaries, where they sleep all day and forage for food at night, feeding on small insects and berries.

Proud of their unusual national emblem, New Zealanders don't mind in the least being referred to as kiwis—and the birds don't seem to have any objection either!

Legacy of
PASSION

BY CATHERINE KAY

A love story begun long ago comes full circle…

Venice, 1819: Contessa Allegra di Rienzi, young, innocent, unhappily married. She gave her love to Lord Byron—scandalous, irresistible English poet. Their brief, tempestuous affair left her with a shattered heart, a few poignant mementos—and a daughter he never knew about.

Boston, today: Allegra Brent, modern, independent, restless. She learned the secret of her great-great-great-grandmother and journeyed to Venice to find the di Rienzi heirs. There she met the handsome, cynical, blood-stirring Conte Renaldo di Rienzi, and like her ancestor before her, recklessly, hopelessly lost her heart.
